COSCOM
ENTERTAINMENT

The Typhon Project

Melinda Marshall

COSCOM ENTERTAINMENT
WINNIPEG

ISBN 978-1-927339-95-4

Published by Coscom Entertainment

Text set in Garamond
Printed and bound in the USA

For Uncle Tim. Just hours before a drunk driver stole him from us, he sent me one last message. "We are proud of you Mindi. Way to go!!!"

The Typhon Project

1

Genetic Kool-Aid

A PIECE OF advice—don't survive the end of the world.

This was my last treatment before The Change. Two needles down. Two more to go.

Medical tape fastened an I.V. tube to the back of my right hand. Thick armrests on a vinyl upholstered chair supported both of my arms. I glanced around the sterile room; fluorescent lights glinted off a light grey countertop and matching tile floor.

The nurse placed a cotton ball on an alcohol dispenser and pumped. I wrinkled my nose at the acrid scent. "The good news is this is your last treatment." Her shoes squeaked against the shiny floor as she pivoted toward me.

She sat on a rolling stool and then leaned in and scrubbed the alcohol-soaked cotton ball over the skin on my wrist just below the thumb. The veins on the back of my left hand have been tough to find after so many treatments. Her wispy blonde hair fell forward. She attempted pushed it back behind her ear, no doubt out of habit. The ear that should have been there to catch the strands was missing; nothing but a stub of cauliflower and a hole remained.

It's funny how you don't notice anyone's ears until they're gone. At first, it shocked me to see people with missing pieces, these pieces they could live without hacked it off to give a few more months of life, a few more weeks of useful service.

She twisted the cap off another I.V. needle and felt around for the vein. My stomach tightened. I turned my head away to stare at a poster of a kitten toying with a ball of yarn, drew in a deep breath, and held it.

"Just a little pinch, Leah," she said.

Why did they always say that? A needle piercing my skin was not a little pinch. I focused on the kitten's pale blue eyes.

Pain struck my wrist, then the faint sensation of the needle sliding in. Stars speckled my vision as the needle sunk deeper. I closed my eyes, drawing a long breath through my nose. I slowly blew the breath out of my mouth.

The hiss of medical tape told me the hard part was over, so I opened my eyes. The nurse fastened the needle down. "Are you okay?"

I blinked hard. "Yeah, I'm fine." The kitten image blurred and doubled; four icy eyes instead of two.

She patted my arm. "That was the last one. You never have to do this again."

She pulled out a syringe full of liquid and exposed the long needle. She inserted it into a receptacle on the I.V. line. It wasn't piercing my skin but the image of the needle set my vision narrowing and turning grey around the periphery. My hands and feet went cold and sweat dewed on my forehead. Within a couple seconds, it was over and she pulled the needle out.

"How are you doing?" the nurse asked.

I couldn't answer; I was too busy trying to stay conscious. I breathed deeper and faster, but seemed to be sliding sideways.

She touched my shoulder. "Leah, are you okay?"

I was in a tunnel, and it was getting narrower by the minute. "I'm not feeling very well." Exhaustion poured over me. I wanted to close my eyes. It would have been so easy to just slip out of consciousness, but I fought back.

The nurse pushed my head down. "Put your head between your knees."

Water gushed on the other side of the room, and then a cool clothe eased over the back of my neck. The dizziness began to pass, my vision clearing. I stared down at my dirty white sneakers against the industrial tiles. I filled my lungs and blew the air out. Slowly, my vision sharpened.

I pulled the cloth off my neck and sat up.

The nurse stood at the counter, tapping something into a laptop. She peered back at me. "How are you feeling now?"

I held the cloth out to her. "Much better."

She took the cloth and tossed it in a hamper. "Just sit back and relax. You've got a little while to go on those I.V.s. Do you want a tablet?"

"Sure." They don't allow us to take our phones into the treatment rooms. No selfies. No sharing the process that goes into The Change on social media.

She took a tablet from a cabinet drawer, handed it to me, and strode out of the room. I looked at my watch, at its double faces, one large circle and one smaller circle both fixed onto a wide leather band. The larger of the two read 12:15. The smaller face held a needle that drifted around the circle, meandering like a lost puppy. A long time ago, it pointed north. Back when it was worn on a much larger wrist than mine.

The tablet was loaded with a bunch of outdated games and only allowed access to a limited variety of websites. There was a history site I'd found last time I was here, full of pictures from before everyone's lives irrevocably changed. I liked looking at old pictures of celebrities, smiling and sparkling. How would those beautiful faces look ashen-skinned and dotted with lesions? Some were probably able to buy The Change, but only some. No amount of money could buy The Change for others who the Human Preservation Agency deemed ineligible.

Most were probably dead. I flipped through images. Dead. Dead. Dead. All those happy smiling faces. Dead.

I glanced up at the plastic I.V. bags hanging above me. The one on the left dripped clear liquid while the one on the right dripped a vivid orange liquid that reminded me of orange Kool-Aid. If only I could squeeze the bags to make them go faster.

Footsteps tapped toward me. "Did you read the information we gave you last time about your final treatment?" the nurse asked.

I looked her in the eye and lied. "Yeah."

She inspected the orange Kool-Aid bag. "Do you have any questions?"

I brushed my thumb over my watch glass. "Will it hurt?"

She lifted her chin. "People experience varying levels of discomfort but most say it doesn't hurt. You should expect some itching. Go ahead and scratch; it will make it all go faster. Some have experienced some mild nausea. If there is any bleeding, make sure to call in immediately."

"How long until . . . ?" I swallowed hard. Until I wouldn't be me anymore.

"It varies. You could start to see changes within the next couple hours, or it may take up to two weeks."

I continued to flip through images and read short articles until my backside ached from sitting for so long. Once the last drops of liquid slid down the tube and into my veins, the nurse extracted the needles.

Weeks and weeks of treatments completed. Finally! I smiled to myself and breathed a sigh of relief.

She bandaged the insertion points and then keyed something into her computer. "Looks like you're good to go. That is, if you're feeling up to it."

I eased myself out of the chair and carefully stood. "I think I'm good."

Continuing to tap on her computer, she said. "Well, then you're free to go." She flashed me a brief grin then returned her gaze to the computer.

I stepped toward the door.

"Oh, Leah?"

I stopped short and tensed.

"Don't forget that you need to meet with your counsellor before you go."

I clamped my teeth together. "I really need to get home. My mom and sister . . ."

"You know the drill. It's required. And it won't take long."

Shoulders slumped, I stalked out of the examination room and down the hall. They were forcing me to see her again. I'd rather have another series of needles.

When I reached the end of the hall, I flung open the door to the north wing of the building, THE TYPHON PROJECT – HUMAN PRESERVATION AGENCY etched into the glass. I looked up the name Typhon when this all started. It's a creature from Greek mythology—a half-reptile, half-human creature powerful enough to defeat Zeus.

The name didn't make me feel any better about my future.

I walked another hall to a bank of three elevators. I pressed the up button and the doors in the middle opened. I stepped inside and selected the seventh floor. Another hall and I found my counselor's office. The receptionist glanced up at me as I stepped inside then looked back to her screen. I plopped down on one of the waiting room chairs covered with a tan, scratchy material. The plaque on her door read DR. NEILA RAIL, B.A., M.A, PH.D. Maybe she should get more letters behind her name.

A pan pipe and a guitar quietly played in the background. I picked at the edges of my bandages then smoothed them back down and turned my attention to a bursting seam on the chair's arm and picked at it. This was stupid. I needed to get home. I didn't have time for a touchy feely with a shrink. I stood and eyed the door to the hallway.

Dr. Rail's office door opened, and I froze. The most hideous creature imaginable stood in the doorway. "Leah, come on in."

2

Psycho Babble

I FOLLOWED DR. Rail into her office, and she closed the door behind me. She wore a wig of white hair in tight corkscrew curls that bounced as she strode farther into the room. She left the sharp scent of designer perfume in her wake. The alcohol from the treatment room smelled better. She directed me to a chaise lounger, but instead I sat in one of the less comfortable chairs in front of her desk. I planned on getting out of here as quickly as possible.

Dr. Rail rounded her desk and eased her weight onto a high-backed leather chair that she scooted closer to the desk. She folded her hands over the glass surface. Her deep crimson nails glinted as though she'd just dug the long daggers into her last client's jugular. "So how have you been doing since I saw you last?"

"Same."

"How are your mother and sister doing?" The fine silvery scales of her skin pivoted and folded past each other as she spoke. Her lips sported the same gory red as her nails. It looked like someone had put lipstick on a fish.

I sighed. "Same."

She leaned back in her chair. "Their condition hasn't deteriorated?"

I rolled my eyes. "What do you think?"

"How about your boyfriend?"

I shifted in my seat. "He's not sick."

"Really?" She raised her eyebrows. "Well, you should be prepared. It's only a matter of time."

I peered past her out the window at the night sky and the dark city below. My anxiety rose with each passing minute. "My mom and Lindsay are alone. I need to get home."

Dr. Rail pursed her lips. "Perhaps if you were more forthcoming this would go faster."

I glared at her. "What do you want to know?"

"I want to know how you're feeling." She pressed her lips into a tight line.

I curled my right hand into a fist and the bandage pulled at my skin. "I told you. I'm fine."

"I have trouble believing that. You're losing everyone you care about and you're fine?"

"Why does it matter?"

"We are as concerned about your psychological health as we are about your physical health. This is a big change and can be met with emotional distress. My job is to help ease your transition."

I rose to my feet. "I'm leaving. I don't have time for this."

She stood and straightened her blazer. "You know, everyone here has lost their families and friends. There's no shame in admitting you are sad or angry."

I clenched my teeth and trembling broke out in the pit of my stomach. I've always tried to keep my emotions bound and gagged, but something was breaking through—a burning sensation in my chest. Like acid around my heart.

I glowered at my counselor. I hated everything about her—her amber eyes with cat-like pupils, her smug smile, her pressed suit. Her skin, especially her scaly skin.

"You want to know how I'm feeling? Like shit!" I shouted. "My sister doesn't even know who I am half of the time, and my mom can't even get herself to the bathroom. Her pee is black. Black! They're dying. And I have to watch! So, what the hell does it matter how I'm feeling?"

A patronizing grin tugged at the scales on her cheeks. "Now we are getting somewhere."

I stared at her, shaking. All the emotion I'd tried so hard to hide hit me in torrents. I beat it back. Falling apart was not an option.

Dr. Rail lifted her chin. "You know, you don't have to watch them die. We can take you to The Farm whenever you're ready."

I folded my arms. How could she even suggest such a thing? "I'm not leaving them."

She raised her brows. "That's your choice, but I hope our talk took some weight off your shoulders."

"Yeah, thanks. You know, I feel so much better now." Sarcasm dulled my voice. I turned on my heel and darted out the door. I took the elevator to the ground floor and made my way to the lobby where I hurried toward the desk near the exit doors, past a row of metal detectors at the entrance.

When I first started my treatments, at least a dozen armed security guards protected the entrance from the desperate. Now there aren't enough people left in good enough health to try to force their way in, so Odin is the only guard left. A crawling baby could force its way past Odin.

He slowly pushed his weight off a creaking office chair as I approached. "Hey there, Leah. All done?" The end of his nose was missing but three discolored spots dotted what was left.

"Yeah, done for good."

He nodded. "Good for you. You're one of the last ones. I guess I won't be here much longer." I couldn't tell if he meant he won't be at this job much longer or at life much longer. He took a box out from behind the desk and pushed it toward me. "My grandson made it to the third round, but got cut in the fourth."

I took my phone out of the box and pushed the box back toward him. "His name was Cole. He was a bright kid, a good kid." He nodded then scratched his nose.

The word "was" seemed to wrap around me. I would have traded places with him if I had the option, though to say that sounds ungrateful. Everyone wanted what I had. Everyone wanted a chance to live. So, I said, "I'm sorry," instead.

Odin blinked a couple of times. "Well, you're a bright kid too. And a good kid. You live for all of us, Leah."

I clutched my phone tighter. "I'll do my best."

He glanced sideways. "Your car is here."

I shoved my phone in my pocket. "Thanks, Odin. Have a good night."

I strode toward the door. My hand on the brass handle, I glanced back at him. He waved, his eyes glassy. I swallowed hard and pushed the door open. Cool night air, tinged with smoke blew past me, then I climbed into the back seat of a white sedan.

The driver, a guy in his thirties who seemed too frail to sit upright, glanced at me in the rear-view mirror then accelerator forward. He drove east out of downtown, past boarded-up and burned buildings.

The driver paid no attention to the faded yellow lines on the pavement. These streets used to be clogged with traffic. Now the entire road was ours.

We passed under a canopy of tall elms lining the streets, the moonlight exposing their once-lush foliage now brown and withered even though summer was still in full swing. Skeletal shrubs, lacking their leafy skins, and crisp, dry grasses lined the boulevards. Tinder for the next fire.

What wasn't already dead was dying.

Just like what remained of humanity.

Streetlights hung over us, as dead as the trees. A solar storm had knocked out the power grid months ago. At least they managed to fix some of the cell towers. Until the next solar storm, at least.

We crossed a bridge that spanned a once mighty river. The wide muddy waters from my childhood flashed in my thoughts. Now, only a narrow stream of water trickled between cracked, desiccated earth.

I eyed the speedometer from the backseat and rubbed my fingers over Dad's watch. My heartbeat spiked to vicious thuds, growing more savage with every passing minute. I wanted to be home an hour ago. "Could you drive a little faster?" I asked the driver.

"Sure thing."

My phone vibrated in my pocket. I checked the time then the message. Graeme's name lit the screen. I grinned as I read his message. *We still on?*

I debated for a moment. It was two in the morning, and I needed at least an hour to attend to Mom and Lindsay. I tapped out my answer. *3:30?*

It didn't leave as much time as I would have liked before sunrise, but it was better than nothing.

His reply came seconds later. *Perfect!*

The driver turned into my neighbourhood, passing my high school. Or what used to be my high school. I would have been starting grade twelve in a month if they hadn't closed the school in December due to a shortage of teachers and students.

The dark two-story brick building lay like a corpse amongst blackened trees. All the first-floor windows were broken. The arched gym roof was charred and pocked with gaping holes from a solar flare that had battered it a few months ago.

Memories of that place seemed like a dream now. I'd stood on the stage in that gym alongside nine other students. Parents and friends sat in folding metal chairs, eyes wide, as we all waited for the results. Only people under 19 years old were allowed to compete. They deemed young bodies the most likely to survive the genetic alterations. Multiple rounds of tests and interviews, each more difficult than the one before, narrowed the competition. As the magnetic field thinned, so did the number of students in the competition, until they reduced us to ten finalists from the entire district.

Every district had been allowed one winner. One survivor. There was no second place.

Dr. Rail had stood at the podium, a cue card pinned between her fingers. She had drawn a breath then read the card. "Leah Baines." The name echoed around the gym. For a split second, my heart raced with triumph. I won! And then my gaze swept the audience. My mom smiled and tears glistened on her cheeks, but every other face blankly stared up at me.

When a whimper had broken the silence, it had hit me. By choosing me to live, all the others had been chosen to die.

The Typhon Project

In the end, seven of us from a city of 800,000 were approved for The Change. Seven people would survive.

Seven.

Across the entire country, a grand total of one thousand were chosen to be the remnant of humanity. If you could still call us human after The Change.

The driver stopped in front of my house. I climbed out and, as soon as I slammed the door shut, he sped away.

The house, windows dark, loomed before me. What would I find when I stepped inside? Were they still alive?

3

Million-year-old Light

I PUNCHED IN the garage door code, but the keypad didn't light up and the door didn't budge. I didn't bring my key. I huffed out an exasperated sigh, then hurried around the side of the house and through the gate into the back yard. The generator silently sat on the patio.

I should have checked the fuel level before I left. How long ago had it stopped? Hopefully Mom and Lindsey didn't wake up and need to turn on a light. I checked the gas tank. Empty. I retrieved the gas can, refilled the generator, and got it humming again. Through the window, the light in the oven hood came on.

Back at the front of the house, I entered the garage door code into the keypad and the door yawned open. I stopped on the step and hit the button to close the door. My hand on the doorknob, I pressed my eyes shut and whispered a prayer: "Please let them be alive."

I knew the day was coming . . .

Refusing to finish the thought, I opened the door and stepped inside. The mantle clock ticked through the silence. It smelled like home—a hint of vanilla mixed with lemon dish soap. For a moment, I imagined I was just coming home late from a date, that I was just a normal teenager. Maybe I'd get grounded for coming in so late.

The Typhon Project

That's the way it would've been if daylight didn't bring the terror of radiation and scorching solar flares. Now night was the only safe time to go outside.

I crept into the living room to check on Mom first. She lay on the couch, sleeping right where I'd left her. She'd slept there since we lost my dad. She refused to sleep in her bedroom. She said it smelled like him. After five years, his clothes still hung in the closet.

I stepped closer. Was she breathing? A shock of panic rolled through me. I tensed and watched her, tears pricking the corners of my eyes. Then she stirred. I let out a breath. I gently tugged her blanket up over her shoulders.

Upstairs, Lindsay's TV flickered. Curled up in her bed, her chest gently rose and fell. I took the remote out of her hand and turned off the TV. I paused to enjoy her face, smooth and peaceful with sleep. When she slept, she still looked like the sister I grew up with—happy, bubbly, easy going. Everyone loved Lindsay. I had looked up to her. She had been a kind and gentle person.

The brain tumors changed her.

She deserved to live more than I did.

I descended the stairs, passing a collage of family pictures decorating the wall. I often stopped to look as I passed; I needed to remember how they used to be before cancer ravaged their bodies.

In the kitchen, I warmed up some chicken broth in the microwave, then set out two trays and filled them with a plate of Saltine crackers, a bowl of chicken broth, and a glass of diluted apple juice. I carried one tray to Lindsay's room and set it on her nightstand and brought the other to Mom and eased it onto the coffee table, careful not to wake her.

"Hi, baby. You're home," she said, just above a whisper.

"Sorry I woke you."

"That's okay." She pushed up on one elbow, but grimaced and fell back onto her pillow. "How did the last treatment go?"

"I didn't faint this time." I chuckled.

"Well, that's good. Now that you've got the hang of it, it's over."

I helped her sit up, placed a pillow behind her back, then set the tray on her lap. She lifted a Saltine to her mouth and bit off the corner. Lesions peeked out from the collar of her nightgown. I watched her chew, willing the cracker to add some weight to her. She was nothing more than a sheet of grey skin draped over bones.

"Mom, would you mind if I went for a drive with Graeme? Maybe just for an hour. "

"I don't mind."

"If you don't want me to, that's okay."

She swallowed. "No, you should go."

"I shouldn't go. I-I shouldn't leave you guys." I pulled my phone from my pocket. "I'll just text Graeme and let him know."

She placed her hand on my knee. "Sweetie, we'll be fine. Lindsay is sleeping. I'll go back to sleep." She sighed. "We're just fine. Go."

"But if Lindsay wakes up . . ."

She lifted her chin. "Leah Marie Baines, you better go out with that boy or you'll be grounded." She smirked. "You need to have some fun every now and then."

"Are you sure?"

Mom rolled her eyes. "Leah. Go."

"Call me if you need anything, and I'll come straight home."

"It's not like the world is going to end while you're gone." She let out a weak chuckle.

I raised my eyebrows. "Very funny."

―――――――

Graeme's old chevy rumbled down the dark highway. He rested his arm on the open window and the wind ruffled his black hair. He glanced over at me and smiled. His dimples. My gosh. His dimples.

I slid down the bench until I could lean against him. Being with Graeme was a vacation from reality. He wasn't sick yet, so it was easy to pretend the world wasn't ending.

I leaned my head on his shoulder. Was he okay? He always told me not to worry, but I did anyway. His younger brother, Liam, the last of his family, died a couple of weeks ago so Graeme was on his own now.

But we agreed not to speak of the dead and dying when we were together. Vacation from reality and all that.

He took an off ramp into the nature reserve. We sped past shadowy, stick-like birch trees. He drove through the parking lot and then down the walking path right to the edge of the sand that bordered the remains of a small lake. I grabbed the blanket off the back of the seat as we got out of the truck.

Graeme stood on the sand, his hands on his hips. "Wanna go for a swim?" He grinned.

The lake, now more like a puddle, reflected moonlight off its shallow waters. "I don't think we'd both fit." I laughed, though the sight set off an ache in my chest. I pressed my eyes closed and images of a healthy Lindsay and I splashing each other on brilliant summer's day played in my thoughts.

Graeme tugged at the blanket, pulling me back to the present. He helped me spread the blanket over the sand, and we both dropped onto it. He lay next to me, his hands behind his head. I leaned back on my elbows and gazed up at the stars. I'd learned that it took the light from some of those stars millions of years to reach Earth. Maybe if I got far enough from the Earth, I could look back at our planet and see it as it used to be. For a moment, the lake was full and the leaves were green. A breeze blew past me, raising goosebumps even though I wasn't cold.

Graeme inched closer. He pointed out constellations and when he couldn't find anymore, I started making some up, and then we both stopped talking. The breeze murmured past. One of the great things about Graeme— we could just be silent together without it feeling awkward.

Graeme sat up and turned to face me. He gazed into my eyes, a heavy burden behind his brown eyes, and said, "There's something I need to talk to you about."

I didn't want a heavy conversation; I just wanted to enjoy being with him—free and easy. I sat up too, faced him, then lightly kissed him. "Do we have to talk?"

I tried to kiss him again, but he pulled away. Moisture glistened in his eyes.

My breath caught. "What's wrong?"

He pressed his lips together, blinked a couple times, and looked away.

Tears blurred my vision. "No."

Staring at the lake, he said, "We knew it would happen sometime."

"How bad?"

He sat up, peeled off his T-shirt, then returned to my side. He took my hand and placed it on his side, just below his armpit. Trembling, I pressed down and slid my hand along his ribs. Lumps. Some bigger, some smaller. The bigger ones had to have been there for a while.

And he didn't tell me.

I looked down at my fingers as though hoping the problem was with them and not with Graeme. I could still feel it on my fingers. My throat constricted. "Why didn't you tell me?"

"Telling you wouldn't help anything. Last thing you needed was more to worry about."

Tears tumbled down my cheeks.

"Leah, don't cry. I don't want to spend our last time together like this."

"Last time—you might have months left!"

He dug into his jean's pocket. He withdrew his hand, held his fist out to me, then uncurled his fingers. The Red Pill sat on his palm.

I recoiled from it. No, no, no!

4

A Kiss Between Lies

I LOOKED AWAY from the Red Pill in his hand. My chest tightened and my heart drummed.

He said, "I want you to be with me . . . when I . . ."

"When you kill yourself."

His shoulders slumped. "When I pass peacefully from this world."

"You want me to watch you die." My voice trembled.

"I'm going to die anyway. And it's going to be awful and painful. And no one is left to take care of me. I'm alone."

My throat burned. "Alone? I thought I was with you."

"You have your mom and sister to take care of."

"I can take care of you, too. My mom has offered that you could stay with us."

He sighed. "Leah, what's it matter if I die now or in a couple months?"

I let a ragged breath escape my lips and then threw my arms around him, sobbing into his shoulder. He held me tight.

My words came between sobs. "I thought . . . . that maybe . . . I could keep . . . just one person. Just one." I pulled away to look into his eyes. Tears moisten his lower lashes.

I reached down and closed his fingers around the pill. "I'm not ready to lose you." It sounded so selfish, but aren't we supposed to hold tight to the people we love? We're not supposed to be okay with loved ones dying. The world was upside down. "Please, Graeme." Tears flowed down my cheeks. "Please."

He peered down and blinked a couple times.

"Please!"

He met my gaze and placed his hand on my tear-soaked cheek. "Don't cry, Leah. I-I won't do it."

I searched his eyes—so much sadness. "When we get back, you can get your things together and bring them to my place."

"Yeah. Yeah. I'll drop you off, then go get my things together." He stroked away my tears. "Everything is going to be okay."

I nodded and absorbed the words. Everything is going to be okay. I wasn't stupid. I knew it was a lie. But I was into lies. They were all I had, so I clung to them.

Everything is going to be okay.

He gave me a peck on the lips. "I should get you home."

I grabbed a handful of his shirt and tugged him back to me. I kissed him. "Can't we stay just a little longer?"

He glanced toward the lake puddle and sighed. "Of course. Of course we can." His lips touched mine, soft and gentle, but then turned firm and needful.

I slid my hand up his arm and rounded it over the soft skin on his biceps.

He combed his fingers through my hair. I dragged him with me as I fell back onto the blanket. I threw my leg over his thigh. His hand trailed over my hip to the small of my back, and he urged me closer.

Afterward, I laid in the safe cocoon of his arms. I took in every sensation—his scent, the sound of his heart beating, his warmth. Something inside me whispered that I might never experience any of it again.

He kissed my forehead.

A hint of deep purple drew an outline of the eastern horizon. Quietly, we dressed then hurried to his truck.

I rested my head on his shoulder; the weight of the world bore down on me. For some stupid reason, I'd continued to hope for miracles, believing Graeme was my miracle and that he would survive. When I lose everyone else, I'd still have him.

I felt the ties between us snapping one at a time.

He pulled onto my driveway. We sat in silence for a few moments.

He grasped my chin and turned it toward him. "I love you, Leah." He placed his warm lips on mine and kissed me. It felt like goodbye.

"I'll see you later. Once you've packed your things?" I asked.

He glanced out the window and then back at me. "Sure." He nodded. "Whatever you want." He peered down at the steering wheel.

I got out of the truck and watched him drive away. I wanted him to look back, but he didn't. He rounded the corner, and then he was gone. I wiped tears on my sleeve and strode through the garage and into the house.

I opened the house door. A wail cut the air. I dashed to the living room. Mom sat on the couch, her brow furrowed with worry.

"Mom, what's going on?"

"Lindsay's crying," she said.

"Why didn't you call me?"

She shook her head.

I climbed the stairs two at a time then followed Lindsay's cries into her room. She writhed on her bed, thrashing at the blankets.

I ran to her side. "Lindsay! Lindsay, what's wrong?"

Her enraged eyes met mine. My heart sunk. Oh no.

"You took them!" she screeched.

I rubbed her leg beneath the blankets. "Everything's okay. Just calm down."

She ground her teeth. "You always take my things!"

I knew better than to deny anything; any argument would only upset her more. I had to let her have her delusion. The tumour that ate away at her brain left her beyond reason sometimes. "I'm sorry. I won't do it again."

Her cheeks flushed, and her gaze darted around the room. "You're not sorry! Daddy! Daddy!" She stared at the door as though waiting for him to burst into the room.

"Dad's not here. He's deployed, remember?" I couldn't tell her he was dead. Better to let her believe he was out there somewhere. I wished I could believe that. "He'll be home in a couple of days."

"You're a liar. I hate you!" She lunged at me and I stumbled backward. She grabbed my collar with one hand. The other hand clenched into a fist. She swung. I turned my head away from her blow. She swung again, but caught me on the cheek. The blow rang in my head. I pushed her away and pressed my palm to my stinging cheek.

Lindsay's face fell, and the angry color drained from it. Her bottom lip quivered, and then she broke into crushing sobs. "I want my daddy." She whimpered, her face soft and innocent.

"Me, too. He'll be home soon," I said. "Everything's going to be okay."

Everything is going to be okay.

I eased her head down onto her pillow and covered her with a blanket. I kissed her on the forehead and then I went to the kitchen, put some ice in a washcloth, and pressed it to my cheek.

I swallowed back my tears. She didn't mean it. She didn't know what she was doing. I leaned against the counter while the ice eased the throbbing in my cheek. That was when I noticed the golden hue reflecting off the stainless-steel fridge.

I dropped the ice pack in the sink and grabbed the handle on the heavy shutter. It rumbled as it rolled down its track to cover half the window. I pulled another from the other side and a bang rang out as it met the one on the opposite side. I dashed from room to room, sliding the shutters over the windows until all of them were covered.

With Mom and Lindsay both asleep again, I fell into my bed and pulled the blanket over me. I took deep, calming breaths and focused on releasing my anxiety like Dr. Rail had instructed so many times. My pulse calmed and sleep washed over me.

A long, high moan woke me. Lindsay again? No. Something else. Something familiar. My foggy brain was reluctant to wake; I needed to sleep longer. I checked my watch. I'd only been asleep a couple of hours.

"Leah!" Mom's panicked voice carried from downstairs. Panic?

Sirens! I jumped out of bed.

I had about eight minutes to get everyone into the shelter before the solar flares hit.

5

Pill Bottles and Fingernails

SOLAR FLARE SIRENS wailed. I bolted from my room and stumbled down the hall to Lindsay's room. I flung open her door. The muted TV flashed. "Lindsay, wake up! We have to get to the shelter." I hurried to her bed where she lay facing away from me. She didn't stir. I shook her. "Lindsay!" Her body limply shifted with each shake. I wasn't strong enough to carry her down three flights of stairs. "Lindsay!"

I flung off her blanket and rolled her onto her back. Her head lolled toward me. Her vacant eyes stared past me. I gasped. "Lindsay?" A stream of vomit dribbled from the corner of her pale lips. I shook her again. "Wake up!" As I shook her, something fell to the floor. I scooped it up. An empty prescription bottle. My breath caught. It was a bottle I'd never seen before. I read the contents.

The Red Pill. How did she get this? I dropped the bottle as though it were as poisonous as the pill inside.

"No." I shook my head. "No! You can't do this to me." My voice cracked. I pressed two fingers against her neck, desperate to feel a pulse. "Lindsay, please. Wake up."

"Leah, hurry!" Mom called from downstairs.

I slid my fingers to another spot on her neck and waited for her jugular to pulsate. Waited. And waited.

Nothing. Only her cool skin beneath my fingertips. I stepped back and my hand fell to my side. Tears blurred my vision as I stared at my sister's lifeless body.

"Leah! You have to come now!"

I roughly combed my fingers through my hair and grasped handfuls. My Lindsay. She was gone. Who cared about the solar flares? Let them burn me alive.

"Leah!"

I backed away from Lindsay. Mom called out for me again. I covered my face with my hands and sobbed.

"Leah, please. You have to leave Lindsay." Mom's voice was thick with emotion this time. Mom. Maybe she wasn't ready to burn, but how could she tell me just to leave her here? I scrubbed away my tears.

I dashed down the stairs. Mom, leaning against the banister, watched me descend the staircase.

I couldn't tell her about Lindsay, not now. I forced every thought from my mind but one—get Mom to the shelter. I could save at least one person today.

I slung Mom's arm over my shoulder and wrapped an arm around her waist. Her hip bone jabbed into me. She felt lighter than the last time the sirens went off a mere week ago.

I dragged Mom toward the doorway leading to the basement. Her body trembled against me. "Lindsay?" she asked.

I ground my teeth. "She's not coming."

Mom sucked in a ragged breath.

I half-carried-half-dragged her down the basement steps.

At the north end of the basement, I flipped the switch to open the hatch. The lead-lined door slid open to reveal a steep, narrow flight of stairs plunging deeper into the ground.

I stepped into the stairwell and hit the button to close the door. I tripped on the second step but caught myself.

Mom whimpered and clung tighter. "I'm sorry, honey. I can't . . ."

"Mom, stop. You can. We can." I took my time getting down the rest of the steps.

Inside the concrete-walled shelter, I helped Mom down onto the cot to my right then hit another switch and the overhead door folded closed with a loud metal-on-metal clang. The siren's blare became a background hum. A single fluorescent bulb lit the room in dim, greenish light. A damp, musty scent hung on the stagnant air. I shook out the blanket from the end of the cot and spread it over Mom.

I sat beside her on the edge of the mattress. "Are you okay?"

She panted. "Yes, I'm fine."

Lindsay was alone upstairs. Our home could become her funeral pyre. How could I tell my mother that her daughter killed herself? No. She didn't need to know that. She only needed to know that Lindsay was gone.

My bottom lip trembled. "Mom, Lindsay . . ."

She cut me off. "It's okay. I know." She patted my hand and pulled in a quaking breath. "Thank you for taking such good care of her." Mom stroked tears from her cheek. "And she loved you. She was so proud of her little sister."

I held my breath and peered down at the lines on my hands. I couldn't fall apart. Mom still needed me. I fought back tears with every bit of strength I had.

Mom's fingers skimmed my swollen cheek. "She didn't mean to do that. That wasn't her."

"I know."

The siren hummed and the light bulb buzzed. The cot creaked as I shifted my weight.

"How was your date with Graeme?" Mom asked.

Graeme hadn't come back yet. Maybe he was taking his time packing, saying goodbye to his home. He won't be able to come out until the flare passes.

She probably meant to bring up a happy subject to distract me. "Graeme's sick," I said.

She pressed her lips together. "Oh, honey. I'm so sorry."

I glanced away from her and stared at the rough, grey walls. "It had to happen eventually, right?"

"It doesn't make it any easier."

"He's going to come stay with us, though. So I can take care of him." I forced hopefulness into my voice.

I searched her eyes for comfort, but all I found was another face I'd soon lose, too. My heart hurt. I wanted to carve it out of my chest just so I wouldn't have to feel its ache anymore.

Mom touched my wrist. "It's nice to see you wearing your dad's watch."

I brushed my fingers over the watch's glass. "I never take it off. It's a piece of him. I like having him with me."

"He wanted you to have it. It's the last thing he did."

"What do you mean?"

"He put it in the mail, addressed to you, the day before he died."

"He did? I thought it came when they sent us all his things . . . after . . . after . . ."

"It all came in at about the same time, but he had mailed the watch just to you."

The second hand ticked from the four to the five. I looked at Mom. "Why? Why would he do that?"

Mom shrugged. "I don't know. The last time I talked to him he seemed nervous, as if he knew something was coming."

"The plane crash was an accident, though. He couldn't have known."

"Sometimes people get a feeling. All I know is that your dad was one of the best pilots in the world, and it seems strange that he would just crash without something going wrong."

"You don't think it was an accident?"

"I don't know what to think anymore." One corner of her mouth curled up. "I'll ask him when I see him."

I sighed. The background wailing of the siren quieted then came in three short bursts. The all clear signal. This one was shorter than most.

I shuffled to the door and tentatively tapped my fingertips against it. Seemed fine. I gambled at a longer touch. "The door is cool. I think we're okay." I hit the switch and the door peeled open. No smoke. No flames. The flares hadn't touched our house.

I heaved Mom up two flights of stairs back to her spot on the sofa.

Mom moaned as I helped her lie back against her pillow. "Don't worry about calling in about Lindsay."

"No, Mom. I'll take care of it."

"No, I'm her mother. It's my job. I'll call them to pick her up in a couple of hours. They can't come until after sunset anyway."

I twisted open Mom's pain medication bottle. I handed Mom a green pill along with a glass of water. She tossed the pill into her mouth, took a sip of water, and then handed the glass back to me. "I'm going to get some sleep and I want you to get some, too."

She'd get no argument from me. I was exhausted. I pulled the blanket over her, and then dragged myself upstairs. As I passed Lindsay's room, I pulled the door closed and then shambled to my room and collapsed into bed. I texted Graeme. *Almost got your stuff together?*

As I plugged my phone into the charger, an irritating tickle erupted at one of my I.V. needle sites. I scratched it, then sleep pulled me under.

I woke to an uncomfortable sensation. The closer I came to consciousness, the worse it got. Everything was itchy. I scratched my neck, my back, my feet. Pure pleasure washed over me with each dig of my fingernails. Drowsy, I wanted to sleep more, but I couldn't stop scratching. The irritation intensified. I needed more hands so I could reach everywhere at once. Maybe lotion would help.

I rolled out of bed and rushed to the bathroom. I flipped on the light and squinted against the brightness. As my eyes adjusted, I grabbed a bottle of lotion from the cabinet. I squeezed the lotion onto my hand then rubbed it into my neck, but it only made me itchier. I scratched my neck, scraping my long nails over my skin. Oh, it felt so good! I pulled my hand away from my neck, and something hung from my fingertips in long, thin sheets. I touched the thin material with my other hand.

Skin!

My heart pounded and my legs went weak. No. No. No!

6

Torn Like Paper

I STARED AT the bathroom mirror. Long sections of pink skin were missing. Ragged strips hung between partially intact pieces. The normal skin that remained bubbled. Patches of fine silvery scales peeked out between in the strips. I rubbed my neck and more skin rolled up beneath my fingertips as it peeled off.

I skimmed my fingers over the new skin; smooth when I stroked it one way, rough if I stroked against the scales. The itching intensified. The skin on my cheek was discolored, too pale. I balled my hands into fists. I thought I'd have more time before this happened.

My breathing came in rapid, shallow gasps. The air thinned. I sucked air into my lungs until they hurt. I threw my hand over my mouth. I couldn't stop it. I couldn't control it. My head spun. It's disgusting. I don't want this. A high, keening cry escaped my lips. Stumbling backward, I crashed into the wall and slid down it to the bathroom floor. I erupted in convulsing sobs.

The itching tortured me, but if I scratched, it would scrape off what was left of my normal skin.

I'd known the change was coming. I'd seen others who had changed, like Dr. Rail. But to see it happening to me . . . .

Curled up on the bathroom floor, I cried until my tears ran dry. Then I just lay there, staring at the cabinets, barely breathing. I couldn't do this—lose my sister and myself in the same day. And Graeme? What would he say? How could he ever look at me again?

Death. That's what I wanted. To be dead like Lindsay. No more loss. No more suffering.

But . . . Mom was downstairs. She needed me.

I forced myself to stand. I looked in the mirror again. More bubbling skin. More silver scales peeking out from tears in the normal skin. No matter how much I wanted to, I couldn't keep the old me.

Get it over with.

I slipped out of my clothes. My jeans took swaths of leg skin with them.

I climbed into the shower. The warm water poured over me, washing the tears from my face. The water pressure removed some of the peachy pieces. The rest I scoured off with a loofah. Bits and pieces of my humanity slid down the pipe or clumped around the drain.

I ran my fingernails over my scalp, and hair and skin fell to the shower floor. Hair clogged the drain. I pushed a pile of it into the corner with my foot. I wept as the pile of hair grew, and I scrubbed until I couldn't feel any hair left.

The water beaded on the new skin—the Typhon skin. That's what I was now. No longer human. A Typhon like Dr. Rail. My stomach heaved and I vomited into the drain.

I turned off the water, got out of the shower and dried off, using the towel to scrub off any bits of leftover skin. Good thing I hadn't turned on the bathroom fan; the steam coating the mirror shielded me from seeing the new me.

I pulled on some long pants and a hoodie. I pulled the hood over my bald head and tugged the sleeves over my hands, just leaving my fingertips exposed. The sun had set so I went around opening the shutters. Then I cooked Mom some thin oatmeal. I placed her cereal and a glass of milk on the tray and then reached for the second tray but pulled my hand back. Only one tray now.

I froze, staring at the food. I had to carry it to Mom. She would see me, see what I'd become. I didn't want her to see me like this. I rubbed away more tears. I was tired of them. I felt like all I'd done was cry for years. It had started the day Dad died and hadn't stopped since. It was as though when he died, he took all the goodness left in the world with him.

I grasped the tray and, with a deep breath for courage, carried it to the living room. Moonlight cast long, faint shadows on the carpet as I shuffled to Mom's side and set the tray on the coffee table. Her eyes fluttered open. A salt trail ran down her temple, the dried remnants of her tears. "Oh, thanks, honey." She tried sitting up but she couldn't lift her back off the couch. She groaned.

My hand at her back, I raised her to a seated position and propped her up with pillows. I waited for her to notice. I waited for the shock and horror to alight in her eyes. She peered up at me. I hoped the hood hid my face well enough that it would soften the blow. I handed her the bowl and she looked down at my hands.

She tilted her head to try to catch my eyes. "Leah?" She pushed the bowl away, so I set it back on the coffee table. She took my hand, pushed my sleeve back and ran her fingers over the scaly skin. Was she disgusted? She had to be.

She issued a weak smile. "Let's see your face."

"I don't want you to see me like this." My voice trembled.

"I want to see your pretty face."

It wasn't pretty anymore. "No."

"Leah Marie take off that hood right now." Her attempt to make her voice sound severe only made her sound weaker. But when she used my middle name, she meant business.

I sat down next to her on the couch. Swallowing hard, I slowly lifted my hood and pulled it back. I pressed my eyes closed. I couldn't look at her and see her reaction. I couldn't deal with seeing her horror. I didn't even know who I was anymore.

Mom gasped. "Oh, Leah." She touched my cheek. "You're so beautiful." I opened my eyes and searched her expression for a hint of deception but found none. How could she think this was beautiful?

"Turn on the light so I can see you better," she said.

I switched on the lamp on the end table. She brought my hand closer and turned it back and forth. It shimmered in the light.

"It's got the same peachy-pink undertones, but with a silver sheen. And so smooth." Her voice held awe. She had to be lying to make me feel better.

"Mom, it's disgusting."

"No, it's not. You are the most beautiful young woman I've ever seen. And I'm thankful for this skin; it's going to save your life."

I pressed my lips into a tight line. "Maybe I don't want my life to be saved."

"Don't say that."

"I don't want to live without you and Dad and Lindsay. I want to be with you guys. Not alone."

Mom pulled me toward her, and I wrapped my arms around her frail shoulders. "You are going to do great things, Leah Marie. You are going to find a way to fix this problem with the magnetic field, and you have to live to do that. Do you know what it means to me to know you are going to live? It's everything to me."

She pushed me away and wiped my tears with her fingers. Her gaze turned hard, determined. "You are going to live enough for all of us. Do you understand?"

I nodded.

"You are not going to give up! Do you understand?"

My bottom lip quivered. "Yes. Yes, I understand."

"I know this is hard, baby. Go to the hall closet. There's a box on the top shelf. It's a wig. I read that it might help with the transition."

"A wig?" I touched the scaley skin on my head. Would a wig make any difference?

"Just try it. Maybe you'll feel more like yourself."

I nodded, then went to the hall closet and found the box. I took it to the main floor bathroom and slipped it on. It suctioned to my head. I tugged at it and it felt secure. I peeked at myself in the mirror. It was the same color and style my hair had been. I stroked it. It was soft like my real hair.

I returned to mom. She grinned up at me. "Lovely!"

I blinked away tears. I was a lizard in a wig, but it seemed to make her happy. And the feel of the hair on my shoulders was comforting in a strange way.

Mom took my hand and squeezed it. "Now, go get me the phone. I need to call for Lindsay's pick-up."

With a ragged breath, I grabbed her phone off the coffee table and handed it to her. She waved me away.

I went upstairs to Lindsay's room. They would be here to collect her in a couple of hours, and I wanted to clean up before they got here. I didn't want them to see the dirty dishes on her bedside table or her matted hair or the vomit dried to her lips and crusting her blankets. Somehow, I wanted them to know they weren't collecting just a body. She was a person. I wanted them to see the Lindsay I'd grown up with.

I retrieved a clean quilt from her closet. I untangled her from her soiled blankets and then pushed her body to the far edge of the bed. I spread the clean quilt on the empty half then rolled her onto it and spread the other side over the vomit. I wiggled the clean blanket until I had it smooth and straight beneath her.

In the linen closet, I found a wash cloth and then went to the bathroom and wet it with warm water. I washed the vomit from her face and neck and scrubbed it out of her hair. I brushed her hair until it was smooth and silky. Memories of braiding her hair when we were kids plagued me. My tears dripped onto her tresses. I positioned her on her back at the center of the bed and slid a clean pillow under her head. Running my fingers over her eyes, I drew her eyelids down. I arranged her hair around her shoulders and crossed her hands over her chest. She was finally at peace. Sleeping beauty. No one would ever know it was suicide.

I went downstairs and sat with Mom while we waited for them to come. The clock ticked and chimed at the hour and then the half hour. I held onto Mom and she held onto me.

I checked my phone. Graeme hadn't texted back. He was probably just delayed by the solar flare and busy packing. I texted him again and told him that if he packed his things, I could come pick him up after they collected Lindsay. I told him she went to a better place, but didn't tell him how. That would be my secret forever.

I set my phone down and bit my lip as I waited for the ambulance to arrive and for Graeme to text back. What would he think of me? I brushed my fingers over my new skin and shuddered. I checked my phone every thirty seconds just in case I missed the notification, but no texts came in.

A knock echoed from the door. I hurried to the window. An ambulance sat on the driveway. I opened the door and two men stood on my front walk separated by a stretcher.

"We're here for Lindsay Alexandra Baines," the one closest to me said.

Both men had scarred patches on their exposed skin. I motioned for them to come in then closed the door behind them. "She's upstairs."

I led the way upstairs to Lindsay's room. I opened the door and stepped aside so they could get in. One man unzipped the body bag. They positioned themselves, one at her feet and one at her shoulders. They lifted. Her arm flopped down and dangled beneath her. They heaved her onto the stretcher. They pushed her arm and hair inside the bag. I took one last look at her face before they zipped the bag shut.

Goodbye, Lindsey.

They carried the stretcher down the stairs. I stood by the door waiting for them. When they reached the entryway, I opened the front door for them. Dr. Rail stood on my doorstep. I gasped. Why was she here?

I looked back at the men with the gurney, and they fixed an irritated glare on Dr. Rail. She stepped inside without being invited. The men pushed past us and rolled the stretcher down the front walk. I furrowed my brow as they carried my sister away from me.

Forever.

"I'm sorry about your sister," Dr. Rail said. My gaze stayed on the body bag until they loaded it into the ambulance and slammed the doors shut. I watched them drive away and then closed the door.

Then I turned to Dr. Rail. "What are you doing here?"

"And good evening to you too, Leah." She clicked her tongue. "Well, well. Look at you. Aren't you a sight? Your skin is lovely, much better than that weak pink stuff you used to have."

I pulled my sleeves over my hands.

"Oh, Dr. Rail. Please come in." Mom had managed to get herself off the sofa and leaned on the wall for support.

Dr. Rail smiled. "Good evening, Mrs. Baines."

I dashed to Mom's side and shifted her weight onto me her before she could fall. I walked her back to the sofa and eased her down. Dr. Rail sat on the love seat. I sat beside Mom and took her hand in mine; I could feel the outline of every tendon and joint beneath her thin skin.

Dr. Rail leaned forward. "Do you have your things together?"

I narrowed my eyes. "My things?"

"The things you'll be taking with you," she said as though it should be obvious.

Mom squeezed my hand. "Dr. Rail is here to take you to The Farm."

7

One More Red Pill

DR. RAIL CAME to escort me to The Farm? I allowed the words to sink in. No, that couldn't be right. I yanked my hand from Mom's grasp. My throat tightened. "I'm not going yet."

Dr. Rail tilted her head, probably so she could speak down to me more effectively. "Leah, there is nothing more you can do here. Your mother called us this morning to come get you."

I sprang off the couch and glared at Mom. "You called them? No, no! I'm not going. You need me here!"

Mom tugged down on my hand, but I held my ground. She said, "Honey, it's for the best. And I'll be fine. I don't have much longer left."

"I'm staying until . . . until . . ." The words jammed in my throat.

Mom peered down at her lap and sighed.

My breathing hitched. "And Graeme . . . I need to take care of him."

"I'm sorry, Leah, but Graeme is no longer with us," Dr. Rail said.

"What? No. He wouldn't. No!" I began to tremble.

Dr. Rail lifted her chin. "You see, Leah, there's no reason to linger here."

I balled my hands into fists. "Shut up, shut up, shut up! You don't know anything!"

Mom sighed. "Dr. Rail, could you leave us for a few minutes? I'll send her out to the car once she has her things together."

Dr. Rail nodded, stood, and smoothed her skirt before striding out of the room and then out the door.

Tears tumbled down my cheeks. "Why did you call her?"

Mom patted the cushion beside her. "Sit down next to me." She took my hand and, this time, I allowed her to pull me to her side. "I can see what this is doing to you, and I hate that you're hurting all the time. You've been surrounded by the dying for too long. Life is waiting for you, and it's time for you to find it. Leave death behind and move forward."

"But I want to take care of you. Who is going to look after you? I'll worry about you all the time."

She inhaled and then slowly exhaled. "When you leave . . . I'm going to leave, too." She patted the pocket of her chenille bathrobe, and something rattled inside. She pulled out a prescription bottle, twisted the cap and poured the Red Pill onto her palm. "I think Lindsay had the right idea."

I gasped. "How'd you know?"

"Lindsay had a lucid moment. She came downstairs." Tears pooled in Mom's eyes. "She said she was so sorry for hurting you. She told me what she was going to do, and we hugged and said our goodbyes. I told her not to wake you. We both knew you'd try to stop her."

I drew a ragged breath. "How could you just . . . just . . ."

"She was suffering. She wasn't going to get better. She wanted relief." I lay my head on Mom's shoulder. She stroked my cheek and said, "Dad's asleep. Lindsay's asleep. I envy them. I'm tired, too."

I wrapped my arms around her and crushed her into me. She smelled of soap and lotion and—Mom. She smelled like my mom. I breathed the scent in until my lungs were full. "I love you. I don't want to go."

"I love you, too, baby, but you need to. So, be a good girl and go save the world, okay?"

I pulled away and looked at her through tear-blurred eyes. She cradled a strand of my hair on her palm. "Go upstairs and pack your bag and then get me a glass of water before you go, okay?"

I nodded, held onto her for a long moment. She patted the back of my hand. I let go of her then slowly climbed the stairs. My legs were numb. I clung to the railing. After digging a duffle bag out of my closet, I glanced around my room. What should I take along?

I grabbed a family photo and freed it from its frame. I stuffed some of my favourite clothes in the bag along with a medal the Navy had awarded Dad and a picture of Graeme and I at West Beach when it still had all its water. I zipped my bag closed and took one last look around my room before heading for the stairs.

I took each step with intention. I stopped halfway down the stairs and let my gaze roam over the house. So many memories—Christmases, birthdays, lazy rainy days when we played board games together. Dad was a board game fanatic. The piano sat collecting dust in the dining room. Lindsay used to fill the house with such beautiful melodies. I wanted to remember it all—the smell of cookies baking, the tinkle of cutlery against plates during family dinners. Dad's laugh.

I set my bag beside the door and then went to the kitchen to get Mom's water. I felt like I was an accomplice to her death as I filled the glass with the water she'd use to wash down the Red Pill. It was as if I was loading the gun so she could pull the trigger. I turned the water off then shuffled to her side and set the glass on the coffee table.

"Thank you," she murmured.

I eased my weight onto the coffee table across from Mom and studied her. Pain no longer lingered behind her eyes. Peace had come over her features. And determination and . . . joy? Was she really happy with this decision?

I stared at her, trying to memorize every piece of her—the heart shape of her face, the blue of her eyes. I closed my eyes to make sure the image was still there. Yes, burned into my memory. I opened my eyes.

Mom grinned. "Dr. Rail is waiting for you.

I hugged her again. This would be the last time.

Ever.

I buried my face in her hair and breathed deeply, etching her smell into my brain and filing it with the other things I forbade myself from forgetting.

She was the first to pull away. She clamped my face between her hands. Her eyes narrowed. "Live."

I nodded.

"And don't look back when you drive away." She smiled—a wistful, dreamy smile. "I get to see the love of my life soon."

More tears fell. I tried to keep my breathing even. "I love you, Mom."

She kissed me on the cheek. "I love you, too. I'll see you again someday. Now go."

For a moment, I couldn't move. Finally, I forced my legs under me. I walked to the entryway, picked up my bag, and slung it over my shoulder. With the door open a crack, I said. "Bye, Mom. I love you."

"Bye, baby. I love you, too." Her voice broke.

The Typhon Project

I took a deep breath, walked out the front door, and stepped outside into the night air. Crickets chirped. The smell of smoke was thick on the air from the solar flare, which must have set something ablaze nearby.

For the last time, I closed the door behind me.

I stumbled down the walk, my legs like jelly. The driver opened the door, and I dropped into the back seat. Dr. Rail peered over the passenger seat at me and then returned her gaze to the windshield. The driver backed out of my driveway and sped away. And though it caused me physical pain, I did as Mom asked.

I didn't look back.

We passed out of the neighbourhood I'd grown up in, then turned onto the freeway and followed it to the west side of the darkened city. I took one final look at the vacant city. I probably wouldn't see it again. When we turned onto the highway, I lay down on the seat and allowed my tears to fall, my body shaking with silent sobs. Eventually, exhausted from crying, I fell asleep.

Dr. Rail woke me. The sun was up. I startled, and then remembered. Oh, yeah, it's okay for me to be out during the day now. I wriggled my fingers in front of me—my scaly Typhon fingers.

I sat up and looked out the window. Tall, golden grasses swayed in the breeze in front of an old rest stop. Parked in the shade of a graffitied, metal clad building, we were the only car in the lot. I hurried to the women's bathroom, stepping over dandelions that grew between the cracks in the sidewalk. Upon opening the restroom door, something scurried into the far stall, so I chose the first stall. The toilets sported a thick layer of dust, but the plumbing still worked. I peered into the mirror at my swollen eyes as I washed my hands. The hand dryer no longer worked, so I wiped my hands on my pants.

When I returned to the car, Dr. Rail offered me something to eat and drink. I took the water bottle from her but refused the food. We got back on the highway. I watched the scenery whipping by for a few minutes, but there was nothing to see but dead grass and blackened patches of earth, so I fell asleep again.

I awoke some time later, my face glued to the leather seats by drying tears. I peeled myself away and sat up. "Where are we?"

"Just outside of Medicine Hat." Dr. Rail's curls bounced as we drove over a bump. "We're almost there."

I stared out the window. More dried grasses. The soil here was rocky and broken by shallow crevices. It reminded me of pictures of Mars I'd seen. Desolate. Lonely. Dead.

As though she could read my mind, or maybe my thoughts were just clear on my face, Dr. Rail spoke. "You are going to love The Farm. People your own age. The grounds are beautiful. Green and full of life." I couldn't see her face, but could tell by her voice she was smiling.

How could I ever love being with a bunch of strangers? By now, Mom was probably with Dad and Lindsay. And Graeme. Graeme. He was lost in a crowd of people I was grieving. I imagined them all rejoicing together at their reunion, catching up on all that's gone on since the last time they saw each other.

Having a party without me.

What I wouldn't give to be with them and not on my way to The Farm.

Dr. Rail looked back over the seat, an excited gleam in her eyes. "Look! There it is." She pointed forward.

I peered through the windshield into the distance. Something shimmered on the horizon, like a bubble rising into the sky. The closer we got the more the huge dome came into focus. Sunlight reflected off the structure. I squinted.

We drove up to the dome's edge, and the driver slowed the car to a stop. The dome stretched in either direction. Inside, the road continued into the dome as though through a haze. The driver pulled a card out of his breast pocket and swiped it in front of a silver box perched at window height. The box beeped and an apple-sized aperture in the dome appeared in front of us. The opening expanded until a car-sized hole opened.

The driver eased the car forward. I turned around and, through the back window, I could still see the desert wasteland. The circular opening shrunk until the dome sealed shut. I faced the front and gazed at the lush, green grass lined the roadway on either side of us. Ahead, trees covered in jade leaves shaded the shrubs below.

It was perfect and beautiful.

And I hated it.

8

Everything Everyone Else Wants

I STARED OUT the window, my gaze bobbing from tree to shrub to flower. The lush green overwhelmed my senses. How long had it been since I'd seen the world like this?

The car slowly followed a narrow strip of black top shaded by a dense leafy canopy. I focused on an individual leaf, dangling beneath the others, wide near the stem then curved inward to a point. A cluster of evergreens broke up the green canopy, their spires pointing to the silvery shimmering dome overhead. Pinecones dotted the emerald lawn.

Ahead, two- and three-story buildings, all constructed of the same red brick, stood beside the drive and dotted the vast lawn. Ivy clung to the bricks, its tendrils reaching over doorways and white-framed windows. We rounded a curve and passed another cluster of trees and more buildings came into view. They formed a circle around a vast courtyard, and islands of flower beds exploded with vivid reds and yellows. A fountain at the center, sprayed glistening droplets of water from a series of giant marble spheres that surrounded a statue.

The driver stopped in front of a building, all brick and glass. Ivy stretched the entire three stories and then dripped from the eaves. A Typhon girl stood on the sidewalk. I stared at her through the tinted windows. She grinned at me. I caught sight of my reflection in the window then quickly looked away. I saw myself long enough to know that on one side, my bangs stuck out above my forehead, while the other side lay flattened against my skin. I smoothed my bangs down and ran my fingers through my hair. Neither helped much.

The driver and Dr. Rail got out of the car and joined the grinning girl on the sidewalk beside my door. They peered into the car window at me, probably waiting for me to get out. My heart sped and I took a trembling breath.

If only I could go back home—the home I had before Dad died, before the magnetic field gave out.

The driver opened my door, and the heavy scent of moist earth and cut grass hit me. Sunlight spilled onto the back seat. I slid to the other side to keep out of its damaging rays. The girl leaned down and looked into the car. "It's okay. The sun won't hurt you anymore."

"I know," I said, even though I'd already forgotten. How long would it take me to get used to allowing the sun to touch my skin without panic setting in?

Dr. Rail tugged down on her blazer. "You're safe here, Leah. Come on out."

I heaved my bag off the floor and scooted across the seat into the sunlight. The sun's rays hit my skin, bright and warm. I shuddered. How strange to allow it to wash over me.

The brilliant light poured over me as I stepped out of the car. Searing daylight stung my eyes, and I threw up my hand to shade them. They hadn't been exposed to sunlight in so long. Then a sensation slid over my eyes and everything darkened enough to make the brightness more comfortable. I peered at the smiling girl, and her eyes were still visible through the slight haze of her second eyelids. I lowered my hand to my side.

Dr. Rail set a hand on the girl's shoulder. "Leah, this is Parminder. She's going to show you around."

Parminder flashed a toothy smile. "Welcome here, Leah." A slight accent flavored her words. Her skin was scaly and silvery like mine, but a darker shade with brown undertones instead of pink. Her eyes gleamed a golden yellow.

Were mine that color now? I hadn't looked in a mirror since the change and hadn't noticed in the car window reflection.

I nodded. "Th-thanks. Good to meet you." My voice cracked as I spoke so I cleared my throat.

Dr. Rail huffed out a breath. "Well, I'm going to go check in at my office and get situated. Are you okay with Parminder?"

"Yeah, I'm fine." I'd take any complete stranger over Dr. Rail. She pivoted and her black pumps clicked against the pavement as she walked down the sidewalk leading toward the fountain. She strode past a pair of students lying in the shade of a towering tree, books in their hands.

"Follow me." Parminder turned and her glossy black braid swung with her. It was a beautiful wig; it almost looked real. She opened the glass door to the building and motioned me inside.

I hesitated and took a deep breath enjoying every smell—earth, flowers, pine. Memories of playing in my backyard as a little girl, giggling with Lindsay, bombarded my thoughts. A sweet scent drifted on the air. It was so familiar. A flower—one I'd often smelled at my grandparents' place. I searched my surroundings and found the culprit—lilacs. Their lavender blooms waved in the light breeze.

"Beautiful, isn't it?" Parminder said.

"It's so green." I was used to seeing brown everywhere. I couldn't pull my gaze from the beautiful colours. Air cooled my gaping mouth. "How do they keep everything so green?"

"The dome holds in the moisture, and there's an artificial weather system that produces wind and regular rainfall. It rains every Monday night and Thursday night, so you can plan your activities accordingly."

"It rains?" I hadn't seen rain in so long.

"Yes. And it's so peaceful and refreshing." She swept her gaze over the lawn. "I know it's hard turn away from it at first. But I'll show you your room, so you can put your things away. You'll have weeks and months and years to enjoy the outdoors."

I hitched my bag strap higher on my shoulder and nodded.

We stepped inside and the door closed behind us. An archway decorated with an infinity symbol stretch over another doorway.

Parminder lifted her chin toward the arch. "The Typhon Project, which we call The Farm, has four quadrants: Arts, Athletics, Language Arts, and this is the Math and Science quadrant. They've assigned us to each quadrant according to our aptitudes."

"I'm in the math and science quadrant?"

"Yeah, we like to call it the 'geek quad.'" She laughed.

She led me over terra cotta tile and past multiple large, square windows. Sunlight flowed through the windows, warming the room. Four halls ran off the entryway. Parminder strode toward the second one from the right down a long hallway. "We're in Faraday House," she said.

We entered a sizable room. Leather sofas and easy chairs framed a plush area rug. One wall sported a huge TV while bookshelves covered the opposite wall. A boy lounged on one of the sofas, his legs hanging over the arm. Earbuds in his ears, I could barely make out the faint tinsel of music. A girl sat on one of the chairs reading, her legs tucked under her. Her stomach protruded, bulbous on her thin body. Was she pregnant? No, these Typhon bodies probably just carry weight differently.

"Maxine, this is Leah."

The girl with the book, Maxine, looked up and smiled at me.

The boy got up off the sofa, removed his earbuds, and made his way toward us. He didn't seem to notice me. He smiled at Parminder. He sauntered up to her and kissed her on the cheek. A blush spread under her silvery scales. How did her Typhon skin feel on his lips? Seemed disgusting.

"And this is my boyfriend, Drake," Parminder said.

"Nice to meet you . . . ?"

I shifted my bag strap higher on my shoulder and extended my hand. "Leah."

He shook it. "Nice to meet you, Leah."

He released my hand then wrapped Parminder in a hug, but she pushed him away. "I'm in the middle of a tour."

He chuckled. "Alrighty. But I will find you later. Enjoy your tour, Leah." He returned to the sofa and reinserted his earbuds.

She cleared her throat. "They've arranged us into family groups. With you here, there are ten of us in the Faraday family. Five boys and five girls. We look out for each other; we study together and that sort of thing."

The Typhon Project

Two halls led off the family room, one on either side. Parminder pointed to one hallway. "The guys' rooms are over there. Girls are over here."

She hurried down the hallway on the opposite side. I quickened my pace to keep up. She showed me the bathroom, then we continued down the corridor. She rattled off the names of occupants as she passed doors. My head was starting to spin. How was I ever going to keep track of all this? It felt like it was falling out of my brain as soon as it went in.

At the end of the hallway, Parminder opened a door. She motioned for me to go through first.

A double bed topped with a fluffy floral comforter sat at the center of the room. Next to it stood a nightstand with a lamp and an alarm clock. A tall window on the other side of the bed allowed light to pour into the room.

"And this is your room." Parminder opened the closet door. "Plenty of room for all of your things."

I glanced at the closet then the dresser. More space than I needed since all of my possessions fit in a large duffle bag.

Parminder strode over to a wide desk that held a laptop computer. She lifted the screen and turned it on. She slid her index finger over the mouse pad and clicked an icon with a blue block letter T.

"All the project sites are connected online through the Typhon Project Network Interface. That's a mouthful, so we just call it the Tynet. You can use it for research and for talking to students in other projects around the world. There are even some interactive games, if you're interested."

She continued. "You can leave your bag here, and I'll show you around the campus. I'm sure you're tired, so I'll make it quick."

I set my bag on the bed. Tired didn't even come close to describing the exhaustion that seemed infect my bones.

I followed her back down the series of hallways and back outside into the sunshine. I felt the odd sensation of my second eyelid closing and my surroundings dimming, like built-in sunglasses.

We strolled down a winding walkway across the drive from our dormitory. Parminder pointed at a group of three buildings, all five stories tall, on the far south side of the property, beneath the hazy curvature of the dome. "Staff offices are over there, the clinic, and the hospital." She motioned toward a three-story structure with huge windows running from the ground to the second story. "That building is Hawking Hall . . . or geek quad central. Whichever. All of your classes will be there."

She turned and I followed her back toward the huge courtyard. We reached the fountain. A statue rose from the water—a muscular man covered in scales with legs that resembled snakes. Water sprayed from a scepter clutched in his right hand. At its base, beneath the blue water teaming with colourful koi, a plaque read IMAGO TYPHONIS.

We skirted the pond and then Parminder led me down a sidewalk to the right. We traversed an ocean of lawn. A huge building that must have been at least ten stories tall stood in the distance. "That's the Tesla coil. Every Tuesday and Thursday afternoon we have work duties. You must be some sort of physics genius because you've been assigned to work within the coil. Only one other student has been allowed in."

I bristled at the word "genius." If I was a genius, I would've found a way to save Mom and Lindsay. No, I was just as ignorant and powerless as everyone else.

"Let's get you back to your room so you can rest. Plenty of time to explore later." She smiled.

Tired, yes. But it was more than that. More like overwrought. I wanted to be alone so I could process all of this. "Thanks for the tour. But, yeah, I could use some alone time."

Parminder led me back to my room. I stood beside my bed and watched her leave, closing the door behind her.

I swept my gaze over the room. This place. It was perfect. Too perfect. Too alive when I was used to being surrounded by death.

I should have wanted this. I should have wanted to go on with my life and enjoy the beauty here. I mean people would have killed for the opportunity to live and not just to live, but to live somewhere beautiful and perfect. But I didn't want it. I'd never been into perfect. Perfect somehow never felt real. Nothing was ever truly perfect. There were always flaws.

This place had flaws; I was sure of it. It just worked really hard to hide them.

9

Dean Green

THE NEXT MORNING, my pillow was still wet with tears. My eyes opened to a strange room. I closed them tight and wished that when I opened them again, I'd be home.

But the new room was still there, all sparse and clean, like a hotel room.

I flung off my blankets and dragged myself to the bathroom. No one else was up yet so I had it all to myself. I peeled off my wig and hung it on a hook outside the shower stall. I stood in the shower for a long time, letting the warm water pour over me, hoping my sadness would swirl down the drain with the crusty salt from my dried tears. I towelled off. The scales caught on the towel if I rubbed them the wrong way. I shuddered at each prickling sensation.

Wrapped in a towel, I walked to the vanity. I stared down at the white porcelain sink, avoiding the mirror as I brushed my teeth. Before, I would have combed my hair. Not anymore. I glanced over my shoulder at the wig perched on a hook.

Did I want to continue wearing a wig? I reached up and touched my bald head, then yanked my arm down. I glanced at the mirror for a split second before looking away again.

The Typhon Project

I had no idea what I looked like. I needed to stop caring. The outside person will never again match the person I am on the inside.

After retrieving my wig, I returned to my room, dressed, then sat on my bed waiting, waiting for signs of life in the dormitory. I watched the clock. Sunlight pierced the blinds, growing brighter with each passing minute. Finally, doors closed, footsteps scuffed in the hall and voices carried.

What would today bring? Probably more new Typhon faces with names I wouldn't be able to remember.

A knock sounded from my door. I shuffled to the door, opened it a crack, and peeked through the slit. Parminder stood in the hall, her hair hanging in sleek sheets on both shoulders. The scent of soap drifted in. "Oh, you're up," she said. "I just came by to see if you wanted to go get some breakfast."

"Um." Did I? My stomach felt hollow; empty but not hungry. Maybe I'd feel better if I ate? "Yeah, sure."

I followed her to the dining hall. I felt like a lost kitten, always on her heels. I mirrored her as she picked up a tray and slid it along a long counter full of muffins, eggs, cereal, and fruit. I chose a bowl of cereal and a banana; it was easy on the stomach. I sat next to her at a round table with a couple of other students.

Parminder spread butter on a muffin half. "Leah, this is Courtney, Roger, and Carter. They're also in our family group."

I tried to smile, but it fizzled, so I turned my attention to my cereal.

"Where are you from, Leah?" Carter asked. His shaggy blond hair fell into his eyes when he leaned forward.

I looked up from the square bits soaking in milk. "Winnipeg."

"A prairie girl. I'm from Toronto."

They went around the table and all said their cities. Parminder was from Langley and Courtney was from Saskatoon. Roger didn't answer; he just stuffed a forkful of eggs in his mouth.

Carter smirked. "Hey, Roger, aren't you going to tell her where you're from."

Roger scratched along the edge of his black, cropped wig and swallowed his eggs. "You can tell her."

Carter laughed. "It sounds so much better coming out of your mouth."

The whole table silently watched Roger and waited. What could possibly be so intriguing about the city he came from? It's not like he was from the moon. Though, we all kind of looked like we were from another planet.

Roger rolled his eyes. "You guys are so immature." He looked at me. "I'm from Dildo, Newfoundland."

Carter burst out laughing.

I listened to their pleasant chatter about school and about conversations Roger had with other students via the Tynet. I glanced around the dining hall at the other tables full of students. I watched them. I had been around sickness for so long I'd forgotten how healthy people act. I'd forgotten what laughter sounded like . . . and sarcasm. It was what life was like a long time ago before the magnetic field gave out.

A girl strode by, pushing a stroller with one hand and balancing a food tray on the other.

"Are you going to school today?" Courtney asked me.

Parminder swallowed a bite of muffin. "You're welcome to, but you don't have to. No one expects you at school on your first full day here."

I considered it for a moment. I felt drained emotionally and physically. But, then I considered the alternative: a day alone in my room with nothing to think about but my dead family and friends.

"I think I'd like to go," I said.

"Okay, if you're sure. We won't have time to pick up your textbooks until after school."

I kept up my lost kitten routine all morning. Parminder introduced me to the teachers and a bunch of students. I gave up trying to remember names. There were too many.

At lunch, I wandered away from her. I wanted to be alone for a while again to process. My nerves were raw; I felt like the tinder-dry trees back home, as if the slightest spark could set me ablaze. I sat at a picnic table outside the school and watched the other students. Had they all gotten over losing their families already? Were they used to the way they looked now? Was I the only one who couldn't stand to look in the mirror? I wanted to be carefree, to smile and laugh like them, but I couldn't.

Was Mom dead by now? Had they roughly loaded her frail body into a black bag like they did with Lindsay? I swallowed against the lump in my throat.

"Hi, you're Leah, right?" A deep voice drew my attention.

I peered up to see a boy standing next to the table. I forced myself to look at his face. I needed to get used to these scaly faces. He was attractive as far as Typhons go. He had friendly eyes despite the elongated sliver of a pupil. He was one of the few students I'd seen who didn't wear a wig. He smiled.

"Yeah, I'm Leah."

He held out his hand. "I'm Dean. Dean Green."

I shook his hand. "Dean Green."

"Yeah, I know it rhymes. My parents had it out for me or something." He chuckled. "I'm in your family group."

"Oh, okay, it's nice to meet you."

"You mind if I sit?"

"No, go ahead."

He dropped his backpack on the ground, stepped up on the bench, and sat down on the table. "So, how do you like The Farm?"

I shrugged. "Seems nice."

He laughed. "You hate it."

I held back a smile. "I don't hate it."

"Yeah, you do. It's too perfect, right?"

I grinned—a genuine, for-real grin. "Just a little."

"Sometimes I walk around and look for weeds. Just one thistle or dandelion, but there aren't any."

"None?"

"Nope. Just flowers. So, I hear you got assigned to the Tesla coil."

"Apparently," I said.

"You and I will be working together then. It's not as glamorous as everyone makes it out to be. The others think we're discovering the mysteries of black holes or something. Mainly, we're just getting coffee for the scientists."

The more he spoke the more excited he got; his words poured out in quick choppy sentences. I was worried he would pass out from not taking a breath for so long.

"Do you do any online gaming?" His eyes widened.

"No."

"A bunch of us are playing Zombie Epoch. We are the last surviving humans, and we go around killing zombies. You should try it."

"I'm not really into that."

"You would be if you gave it a try. There are three different modes, depending on what you like to do—story mode, combat mode, and full epoch mode that combines both. You can play against people from other projects."

A chime rang out. Parminder appeared beside me. "I see you met Dean."

He jumped off the bench, grabbed his backpack and backed away. "Think about it. It's awesome." He said "awesome" in a stage whisper and pointed both index fingers at me before he turned and walked away.

I shook my head.

"Dean will not rest until he sucks everyone into that game." Parminder chuckled.

In the evening, everyone went to their various activities. I met a boy named Luke and a girl named Taylor, who were both involved with an intramural sports group. I also met Sarah, whose room was across the hall from mine.

My head hurt. Too many names. I wanted the familiar ones—Mom, Lindsay, Graeme, Dad.

Parminder and Drake went for a walk. I'm sure she was tired of babysitting me. I decided to check out the bookshelf in the common room. Dean found me, standing at the bookshelf flipping through a copy of The Outsiders. He invited me to play Zombie Epoch again. I refused. I placed the book back on the shelf, went to my room, and collapsed on my bed.

In the days that followed, Parminder slowly gave me more and more space to find my own way around. After the weekend, I felt more confident in finding what was where. I could find my classes and, more importantly, I found the bookstore on my own. My bookshelf was slowly filling up, giving my room a more lived-in look.

I hadn't realized how much I missed school. I eagerly listened during my classes. They were challenging after not being in school for so long, but it was all coming back to me. Dean was always available to help, which was nice because Parminder was usually with Drake. However, I was usually prying Dean away from his game, but I didn't feel bad about that.

I found out Courtney and Roger were together, but much more so than Parminder and Drake. Courtney even spent some nights in Roger's room. Strange they allowed that sort of thing here. Where I came from adults were always trying to keep boyfriends and girlfriends from being alone together.

Thursday after lunch Dean pushed away from the cafeteria table. "You ready?"

I wiped my mouth with a napkin. "Yep." I stood and slung my backpack over my shoulder.

In fact, I was past ready. My first day working in the Tesla coil. Who cared if all I did was bring scientists coffee. I would get to go inside and see how it worked and meet the brainiacs who were working on it. I jittered.

Maybe in some small way, I could be involved in fixing our world. I couldn't get inside fast enough.

It was too late to save Mom and Lindsay. But maybe I could save someone else, and all of this pain and suffering and loss would have some meaning.

10

My Dream Job

MY HEART RACED with excitement as Dean and I walked the sidewalk toward the tallest building on The Farm. It was a foreign feeling to actually look forward to something.

Dean hitched his backpack higher on his shoulder. "You know what we should do after work duty?"

I tossed my head back. Not again. "Play Zombie Epoch?"

"Yes, we should. I'm glad you suggested it."

"No, Dean."

He nudged me with his elbow. "Come on."

"Seriously, I don't want to play."

"Well, you like to read, right?"

I furrowed my brow. His question had to be a trap. "Yeah, I like to read," I answered slowly, watching his expression.

He swept his hand in front of him. "Then, you'd love story mode. It has excellent storylines."

I rolled my eyes. "I'm not a gamer."

He chuckled. "Well, nobody's perfect, but you can change."

We came to a glass door. Dean pressed his thumb to a black box to the right of the door and the door opened. "You'll get set up in the security system today." He motioned for me to go in first.

We came to a second door. Grasping the handle, he asked, "Are you ready?"

"Um, yeah."

He shrugged. "I'm just making sure."

He pressed his thumb to another black box and a steel door swung open. We stepped inside a huge room. The door closed behind us, and a boom echoed through the room. A series of computers lined the outer circle of the colossal room. Men in white coats sat at some of them and others roamed around inspecting equipment.

At the center of the room, a massive coil the width of a semi-truck trailer spiralled above us. My mouth popped open and I gasped. I peered up, up, up trying to find the top, but it disappeared into the darkness high above me.

"Amazing, eh?" Dean said.

"Wow." Mind blown.

"Dean," a man's voice called out. One of the men in white coats waved him over. I fixed my mouth shut and hurried behind him. The man's brow was bunched together in an irritated glare. "Who is this?"

I took a step backward. Dean grabbed my elbow and pulled me a step closer to the angry man.

The man glowered and shook his head. "Oh, yes, yes, yes. Of course. I received a memo about that."

"This is Leah. Leah, this is Dr. Burns."

I opened my mouth to say hello, but he turned away and dismissively waved his hand. "Take her in the back and get her prints uploaded. And then get me some coffee." Dr. Burns marched toward an apparatus with roughly a million wires connected to it.

Dean turned to me and smiled. "See, glamorous and heroic." He pointed upward. "To the coffee!"

I chuckled and followed him into a room at the back that smelled of burnt coffee. We walked around a long table with mismatched chairs at the center of the room and then passed desks piled with papers and file folders to a long counter with a sink, coffee maker, and a bar fridge. After delivering the coffee to Dr. Burns, Dean scanned my fingerprints and set up my security access.

With some difficulty, Dean pried open a drawer in one of the desks and stuck his hand inside. "I'm about to show you a most important and sacred document. This will be the difference between surviving at the coil or getting kicked down to jock strap duty in the athletic quadrant. Are you ready?"

I nodded. He whipped his hand out of the drawer and, with a flourish, handed me the sheet of paper. The title at the top said GREEN'S THEORY OF FLUID DYNAMICS—a spreadsheet with the names of all the scientists and how they liked their coffee. Black. Cream no sugar. Sugar no cream. Two creams one sugar.

I giggled. "Thanks."

"No problem. I got your back."

Dean showed me around and introduced me to a bunch of scientists who I don't think cared to meet me. I itched to know what all the equipment was for and what they were working on, but Dean cautioned me against talking to them, so I bombarded Dean with questions. He knew what most of it was and tried to explain it, but Dr. Burns shushed us.

A heavy weight settled into the pit of my stomach. Dean had warned me that working in the coil wasn't as great as everyone thought it was, but part of me assumed he was kidding. I thought maybe I'd be able to make a difference working in here, but I was just a volunteer barista.

And since Dean refused to risk me making the coffee, I had nothing to do. The afternoon seemed to stretch on and on.

"What time is it?" Dean asked as he emptied the used coffee grounds from the filter into the garbage.

I glanced down at my watch. Three o'clock? That can't be. I looked closer. The second hand was stalled out over the six. I tapped the crystal, hoping to get it moving, but it didn't budge. The battery must be dead. The compass caught my eye. The needle pointed due north. Odd.

"Leah?"

"My watch stopped." I tapped the crystal again.

"That thing is an antique." Dean glanced down at my watch.

"It was my dad's. I guess the battery gave out."

Dean sighed. "I'll go find a clock. I'm dying here."

When Dean returned, he reported that we worked five minutes of overtime. We both hurried from the building. Dean theatrically fell onto the grass and lay spread eagle in the sunshine. "We lived to tell the tale!"

I laughed and sat down beside him. It did feel good to be out in the fresh air after being in that stuffy back room for most of the day.

After dinner, I went to my room and pulled out my calculus book. I stared at the pages, the numbers and letters blurring. I leaned back in my chair and peered up at the ceiling. I didn't feel like doing calculus. Dad's watch needed fixing anyway. Priorities. Anything connecting me to my family was more important than homework.

The Typhon Project

I unbuckled the band and set the watch on my desk. I rubbed my wrist, which felt naked without the keepsake on it. I slid my thumbnail under the backing and wiggled it open to see what size of battery I needed to pick up.

The stainless steel back popped off and something fell out of the watch and onto the floor. I picked up a tiny square of folded white paper. I turned it over and then, carefully, I unfolded it.

It was Dad's writing. I'd recognize it anywhere.

11

Message from the Dead

I PINCHED THE quarter-sized piece of paper between my fingers. It had to be Dad's writing—the way one curve of the S came to a point so it almost looked like the number five. Dad had sketched a compass in pencil and labeled each direction with the corresponding letter. He drew the compass wrong, though. The arrow pointed south instead of north. Strange. Why did Dad hide a scrap of paper in his watch?

I stared at the paper. Tears pricked the corners of my eyes. Dad. What I wouldn't give for one more hour with him. Or with Mom. Or Lindsay.

I swallowed my tears. My family was gone now. A hollow ache settled into my stomach. After setting the scrap aside, I dug the battery out of the inner working of the timepiece, noted its size, and tucked it back inside.

I picked up the paper fragment and kissed it. "Miss you, Dad." Carefully, I folded it just the way Dad had, placed it over the mechanism, and replaced the backing. I strapped the watch to my wrist. The second hand motored around the face once again. I guess I didn't need a new battery after all. I reset the time and then forced myself to crack my calculus textbook.

The Typhon Project

The days slipped into a rhythm and weeks passed. My days were swallowed up by school, homework, and work duty in the coil, which I always dreaded. If it weren't for Dean, I probably would have intentionally botched the coffee. Jock strap duty would've been more fun.

My relationships with the other girls in my family group remained shallow. Parminder didn't seem to have time for anyone but Drake. Sarah rarely talked to anyone. Her nose was always in a book. Taylor hung out with people from the athletic quadrant. I got the feeling she didn't appreciate being placed with the geeks.

Courtney and Roger were attached at the hip. As the months crept by it became obvious she was pregnant. At my high school, it would have caused a scandal, but no one here seemed to give it a second thought. What would a Typhon newborn look like? All slimy and scaly? Horror movie imaginings of it eating its way out of her belly sprang to mind.

Dean was my only actual friend, and I may have been his only friend, too. His incessant begging for me to play that stupid game made me want to slap him sometimes, but I tolerated it. Friends were hard to come by.

As time wore on, the ache in my chest grew unbearable. I cried myself to sleep every night.

I didn't belong here. I could feel it in my soul.

I zoned out in class. Sometimes I didn't do my homework. I'd sit in my room and stare at it, but never do it. I got called into Dr. Rail's office where she confronted me about my poor performance.

One Thursday, my physics teacher droned on about the motion of charges in a velocity selector. I traced my finger around and around my watch's face. The lights flickered, then cut out. Sunlight poured through the large window. Why did they need the light on anyway?

I looked back to my watch. The compass needle swung and locked into the southerly position. I tapped the crystal, but it continued to point south. The lights flashed on and then the needle drifted again. Strange.

After school, I took the long way back to the dorm. I wanted to be alone. Alone was different than lonely. When I was in the dorm with all those people, but had no one to talk to, that's when the loneliness hit.

It was easier to be by myself. No Parminder making out with Drake. No Dean begging me to play Zombie Epoch. No Typhon faces to deal with.

I strolled all the way to the chain-link fence that stood about ten feet from the dome's edge. Wrapping my fingers around the wires, I leaned against the barrier. I peered through the dome, straining my eyes to get a glimpse of the outside world. The haze of the dome obscured whatever lay on the other side. All I could see were blobs in various shades of brown.

I followed the fence around the compound to the back of the Tesla coil. Slipping off my shoes I plunged my toes into the soft, cool grass and sat down in the shadow of the towering Tesla coil building.

I lay back and smacked my head on something hard. I sat up, rubbing the back of my head. I peered over my shoulder. What did I hit my head on?

I crawled closer. A circular metal plate sat flush to the ground, nearly hidden by the thick grass growing around it. Four thumb sized holes penetrated the rough, dark metal. On hands and knees, I peeked through one of the holes. Cool air drifted through it and brushed my cheek.

Dim light lit a shaft. Ladder rungs descended down concrete walls. What was down there? A tunnel?

I wriggled my finger into one of the holes.

The Typhon Project

The bell rang. Uggh. Dinner with a bunch of scaly strangers.

But if I didn't show up for dinner, I'd probably get called into Dr. Rail's office again.

I stood, brushed the grass off my backside, and strode toward my dormitory. Several paces away, I glanced back to place the shaft in relation to the Tesla coil so I could find it again.

I hurried to the cafeteria, added a burger and French fries to my tray, then found our family group table. I set the tray on the table then dropped into the chair beside Dean. I bit off a chunk of burger.

"Where'd you go?" Dean asked.

I swallowed my mouthful. "Me?"

He stabbed his fork into a tomato slice. "Yeah, you disappeared after class."

"I went for a walk."

His shoulders drooped. "Oh. Like, by yourself?"

"Yeah. Is that a problem?"

"No, I just thought . . ." His shoulders bounced up and down in a trio of shrugs. "Nothing. Never mind."

"Not the game, Dean. Never the game."

He sighed, stuffed the tomato in his mouth, and shuddered. "I hate tomatoes."

"Then why are you eating them."

"They're good for you."

I narrowed my eyes. Dean had a mom. She probably told him to eat his vegetables. A lump formed in my throat, but I swallowed against it. "Hey, you know lot more about this place than I do." I studied my fries for a moment. "Do you know if there are any . . . like . . . stuff underground? Like, say, tunnels."

He laughed. "Tunnels? Here? Tunnels would be exciting. This place doesn't know what that word means."

He took a drink of water and stabbed his fork into another tomato. "But if you like secret passageways . . ."

I rolled my eyes. All conversations with Dean led to Zombie Epoch.

Back in my room, I opened my laptop, clicked the Tynet icon and pulled up a Typhon Project Campus map. No tunnels were marked. Maybe it was just a maintenance shaft. I slammed the computer's lid shut then sprawled on my bed.

It was probably nothing. Just wires and pipes.

I picked up a book and read an entire page without comprehending a word. It's like the tunnel was begging, "Leah, explore me. Please!"

I shouldn't. Nope. Bad idea.

What if it was a tunnel, and what if it led out of here?

The walls seemed to close in around me. Dean's words the first time I met him rang in my thoughts. He'd said The Farm was "too perfect."

I was trapped in paradise.

Shouldn't that have been a good thing?

Did a broken world still exist outside of the dome? The sun scorched world outside seemed more real than anything inside.

I flung off my blankets and pulled on a pair of black jeans and a black T-shirt.

I needed to know where that shaft led.

12

Curiosity and Desperation

MAYBE IT WAS boredom that lured me toward that tunnel. Whatever it was, it was impossible to say no. Dressed in all black, I tied my hair back. I opened the bedroom door and peeked into the shadowy hallway. A dim nightlight lit a circle of tile near the bathroom. The slit below each bedroom door revealed nothing but darkness. Everyone seemed to be sleeping.

I tiptoed down the hall and through the common room, my ears alert to the slightest noise. Muffled sounds echoed down the boys' hallway. I hurried toward the back entrance.

I slipped through the back door into the cool night air and eased the door closed behind me.

My heart thrummed. I made it out!

A slivered moon glowed above me. Crickets chirped, breaking the silence. Equally-spaced lamps lit all the sidewalks running toward the fountain. If I followed the pathway to the Tesla Coil, someone would see me for sure. A figure strode down the sidewalk in the distance. I ran toward the chain-link fence at the edge of the compound.

My lungs filled with cool air as my feet padded the soft grass. There was something comforting about being outside in the dark. Back home it was the only time I left the house, but I hadn't been out at night since I arrived here.

When I reached the fence, I followed it south. The Tesla Coil building loomed ahead, a blocky shadow. I pushed myself faster. At the back of the building, I searched in the darkness for the shaft amongst the sea of lawn. I walked back and forth over the area where I remembered it being. Where was it?

There had to be security cameras on the coil building. Did I dare venture any closer? Two steps, three steps. A few more. That was as close as I could safely go. Another step and I stumbled as the ground was lower than I anticipated. My shoe thudded against metal.

I dropped onto my hands and knees. Dim orange-hued light shone through the holes in the shaft cover. I hooked my fingers in the holes and pulled. Its weight tugged on my shoulders. I heaved and the lid budged. Lifting with my legs, I yanked and the shaft cover popped up and swung open on a hinge.

I knelt next to the shaft and peered inside. A cold, dry breeze blew up the shaft and tussled my hair. The ladder descended down, down, down a concrete tube and disappeared into a black abyss below.

I sat back on my haunches and huffed out a breath. I should have brought a flashlight. Should I go back to the dorm and try to find one? But what if I got caught? I could almost hear the question now—why do you need a flashlight and why are you sneaking out at night? Then they'd send me off to talk to Dr. Rail about my strange behavior.

If there was anything significant down there, like some sort of maintenance passageway, there'd have to be lights. And they wouldn't have a random shaft here for no reason.

I peered back toward the dorm. Was this the end of my grand adventure?

I didn't want it to be.

But it was so dark down there.

I was too old to be afraid of the dark. Don't be a wimp!

Gripping tufts of grass, I backed into the shaft and hooked my foot on the first rung. A few rungs down the ladder, I gazed upward, and considered the heavy hatch. Should I close it? It was difficult to open, but if I left it open, someone may notice. I held onto the ladder with one hand and carefully lowered the hatch closed behind me with the other. It slammed shut with a deep boom that echoed down the shaft. The sound carried. And carried. Until it disappeared. By the sound of it there had to be tunnel down there. The single light that lit the upper shaft grew dimmer the lower I climbed. I cautiously placed my feet. If I fell in here, who knew how long it would take to be found?

The temperate dropped as I descended. How deep did this go?

I dipped my right foot for the next rung, but it scraped a surface. I waved my foot out in a circle. More of the same rough surface.

I clung to the ladder as I slowly lowered my weight onto what must have been the floor beneath the shaft. I looked up at the muted light at the top of the shaft. It did nothing to drive out the darkness down here. I splayed my fingers and searched. They brushed a cold, rough wall. Probably concrete like the shaft. I walked along the wall, feeling my way through the blackness.

My pulse quickened. What if I got lost down here in the dark? I wouldn't let that happen. If I didn't find a light source soon, I'd go back to the dorm.

My finger grazed something on the wall, smooth, narrow and rounded. Plastic, maybe? A coated wire? Maybe it would lead to a light switch.

I followed the small plastic tube for a dozen footsteps. I stubbed my fingers against something hard protruding from the wall. I grabbed it with both hands— a small cold box. Metal, maybe. A circular spot in the middle. I pressed my thumb into the circle.

Lights popped on, one after another down the length of the concrete tunnel that seemed to stretch on forever, the light narrowing to a point. Pipes of varying diameters crowded the ceiling while colourful wires encased in a clear tube ran alongside the pipes. If my sense of direction was correct, the tunnel ran in the direction of The Farm dome. It stretched so far it had to extend under the edge of the dome.

What if this was a way to the outside world?

I glanced back in the direction of the shaft. Should I go back?

If there was a way out, I wanted to know.

I broke into a sprint.

13

The Real World

THE TUNNEL STRETCHED before me, concrete walls, floor, and ceiling. Cool, moist air and a musty, earthy scent rushed past me as me feet thudded against the pavement. Light bulbs in wire cages protruding from the wall lit my path.

I hadn't run in a long time, but it felt good to stretch my muscles. I lengthened my stride. Where did this tunnel lead? Maybe to a dead end? No, it had to lead somewhere. Why else would they build it? I ran down a gentle slope as the tunnel descended deeper underground and then up another slope to draw me closer to the surface.

I slowed to a jog to check my watch. An hour and a half had passed since I'd sneaked out of my room. I had to have been running for at least an hour. My heart was racing and my breathing heavy, but I wasn't tired at all. I was in better shape than I thought. Or endurance was another advantage of this new body. Maybe that's one small thing I could like about it.

I picked up my pace. The tunnel sloped upward again but steeper this time. I watched the ceiling for other shafts that might lead to the surface. I had to be well outside of the dome by now. I'd have to be careful not to lose track of time; I had to get all the way back to the dorm before anyone noticed me missing.

What if the tunnel went on for miles and miles?

What if I'd come all this way for nothing?

I stopped and looked back. How much farther should I go?

Fifteen minutes. If I didn't find a way to the surface by then, I'd turn back.

The minutes motored by. I hurried past dozens of lights and meter after meter of concrete. Everything looked the same. I could be running in a giant loop for all I knew.

Up ahead, the light changed. Instead of the orangey glow, the light had more of a blue hue. I pushed myself faster.

I stopped under the light and gazed up at the ceiling. A shaft ran up to the surface just like the one I'd come down. Had I run in a circle and ended up back where I started? My heart sunk. I climbed up the shaft toward the manhole-like cover. Dim, silvery light filtered through the holes.

Please, please let me be outside of The Farm.

I was running out of time. I climbed faster.

At the top, I pressed at the heavy cover, but it didn't budge. I climbed a wrung higher and put my shoulder into it and pushed with my legs. A metal-on-metal grating and the door shifted. I strained harder and the whole thing lifted. This one wasn't a door at all. More of a cap.

I hadn't run in a circle after all!

I pushed it higher and then shoved it to the side. The night sky peeked through the opening. The moon and a glimpse of the milky way glowed overhead. I pushed the heavy disk farther over. Reaching my hands over the lip of the opening, I poked my head through.

Black top pavement surrounded me. Extinguished street lamps lined the roadway. Moonlight illuminated houses, windows dark. I hadn't opened a hatch. It was a manhole cover. I boosted myself up and out of the shaft. I sat on the edge, my legs still dangling into the hole.

Evenly-spaced houses with driveways leading to double garages ran up and down the street. A block down, the dark outline of a stop sign and more darkened houses.

A neighbourhood. Not so different than mine back home.

A cold wind swirled around me. A stray, tattered, plastic grocery bag danced down the street and caught against the branch of a shrub.

No sign of life anywhere. Not that I expected to find any. I shoved the manhole cover back over the shaft and stood up. One of the houses caught my eye. I crossed the street, walked a few houses down the sidewalk, and stopped.

A chill rippled over me and a deep longing filled my chest. The two-story house looked like mine. It had some stonework accents that mine didn't have, but those were easy to overlook in the dim moonlight. I closed my eyes. For a moment, it was my house. It was daytime and the bus had just dropped me off from school. My backpack hung on my shoulder. Mom was inside starting dinner. Lindsay wasn't home yet. She had volleyball practice. And Dad . . .

My breathing hitched.

I opened my eyes but didn't allow the fantasy to evaporate. It was intoxicating. I strolled up the front path, past the memory of the weeping willow Dad had planted in the front yard, past the pink peonies Mom had tended in her flower bed, full of ants but such a sweet scent.

I stopped at the front door—frosted glass in a dark wood frame. I wanted to go home more than I wanted my next breath. What were the chances it was unlocked?

I wrapped my trembling hand around the cold pewter handle, hooked my thumb on the lever and drew in a deep breath.

I whispered, "Please let it be unlocked." If a God still existed on this broken planet, could He do this one thing for me?

But what if the owner was still here? There had to be some survivors out there. Maybe?

Or . . . what if there were bodies? So many houses had become tombs for the last remaining family member. Like my house would have been if I hadn't been changed.

Maybe going inside was a bad idea. But I didn't care.

I pushed the lever down, the latch clicked, and the door popped open.

I held my breath as I pushed the door open—the door that could have been to my home. I smiled, but tears welled in my eyes. I need to remain alert just in case. I stepped inside onto an area rug. The air smelled dusty and stale, but a background hint of cooking onions still spiked memories.

It was all how I remembered it—the entryway closet and the spot where I slipped off my shoes after school. I pushed off my runners and placed them to the right of the door, where Mom always got after me to put them. I walked farther into the house. "Hello? Anyone here?" I paused and listened. Silence. "Hello, anyone? I'm . . . I'm lost."

So much truth to that statement. I was so lost.

Nothing but more silence answered. I pressed my eyes shut for a long moment to conjure my earlier fantasy.

"Mom, I'm home," I called out. I bit down on my lip. The smell of fresh apple crisp. "Did you have a good day?" I whispered for Mom. "Yes, but I missed you," I said.

I shuffled into the living room. The sofa and love seat were in an L shape in front of a TV. That was all wrong. Mom always said they should be across from each other so people could visit with one another. I put my weight into the loveseat and pushed it around until it faced the sofa. I sat on the sofa and closed my eyes again. "Dad, you're home."

"Hi, baby girl," I said for him. "We got a new National Geographic today. The cover story is about the magnetic field."

I had read that issue with Dad, about how the magnetic field weakens and then flips once every hundred thousand years or so. Not this time, though. It just weakened to nothing and abandoned us.

Savoring the placement of my feet on each tread, I climbed the stairs and peeked into the bedrooms—the room that was mine and then the room that was Lindsay's. In this house, Lindsay's room was a nursery with a monkey decal on the wall and white crib beneath it. A small pile of blankets rested at the center of the crib.

I gasped and backed out of the room. I didn't want to know whether it was just a pile of blankets or if someone small lay forever beneath those blankets. Sometimes parents had died before their babies. I shuddered.

I hurried back downstairs and into the kitchen. Silver moonlight spilled onto the counter from the large window over the sink. The smell of soured milk, rotten eggs, and mould hung in the air. The stainless-steel refrigerator probably housed a science project worth of decay. I opened the door to the pantry. Inside, boxes of cereal and crackers, cans of soup, and packages of dried noodles littered the shelves. Bugs crept in and out of a container of oatmeal.

"Lindsay," I shouted. "Did you eat all the pop tarts?" Pop tarts were our pet argument. They were always an issue—who ate how many, accusations that the other had more than their fair share. My favourite was s'more flavour. She loved strawberry. Mom only bought them as a special treat; she didn't like us eating so much sugar. "I'd give you all the pop tarts if you would come back, Lindsay," I said.

"Don't move," a man's voice behind me.

Adrenaline surged through my system, and I whipped my head to glance over my shoulder. A tall and thin shadow in the doorway. Black metal glistened in the dim light. Someone still lived here! I was an intruder. I stiffened.

"Look straight ahead and put your hands up. Slowly," the man said.

I raised my arms. "I'm sorry. I didn't know anyone lived here. I'll leave."

"Quiet!" Then, he mumbled, "No one lives here."

Feet scuffed the floor, inching toward me. I turned my head a smidge.

"I said don't move!"

I pinned my gaze forward. Footsteps drew closer until they stopped directly behind me. Something jabbed my ribs. The gun.

"If you move, I will shoot you."

I froze while my heart hammered against my ribs. A hand patted me down one side and then the other. Then, the feet scuffed away from me.

"Where are the others?" His voice boomed.

"There's no one. Just me." My voice trembled.

"Turn around slowly."

The Typhon Project

I swallowed hard and pivoted around. I stifled a gasp. A young man, maybe a little older than me, with peachy, smooth skin. He's human! I'd thought those who weren't dead were about to be. But even in the moonlight I could see he was strong and healthy. No lesions. No missing pieces.

As his gaze moved over me, his eyes widened. His mouth popped open and he slowly lowered his gun.

Of course, he was shocked. He was a beautiful, perfect human. I had to be frightening, especially at night. His gaze locked on mine for a moment, and then he shook off his stare and lifted the gun again, aiming it at my chest.

He lifted his chin. "Who were you talking to?"

The back of my neck warmed. He caught me in my fantasy. I glanced sideways. "I'm the only one here."

His eyebrows bunched and he shook his head. "Don't lie to me. I heard you talking to someone. Who were you talking to?"

I pressed my lips together.

"Tell me!"

"Lindsay. I was talking to my sister Lindsay."

He glanced one way and then the other. "Where is she?"

I blinked back tears and sighed. "She's dead." The words dropped like a deflated basketball.

"You used to be human." A statement. Not a question. The words cut me like a jagged scrap of metal—slicing through skin and flesh, past bones and organs, right into my soul. I wanted to tell him—no, shout at him—that I'm still human. I looked over at my hands, at the Typhon skin. No matter how much I wanted it to be true, it was still a lie. I was a Typhon. The man in front of me and I were two different species.

My insides jittered. How long would he stand there and stare at me? I peered down the barrel of his gun and my pulse calmed. I didn't care if he shot me. In fact, maybe that was why I was drawn here—to be put out of my misery. My arms and fingers started to tingle so I lowered my arms.

"Keep your hands up!"

"No," I said, my voice dead.

His jaw muscles tightened. "I will shoot you."

I squared my shoulders to give him a broader target. "Go ahead."

14

Lying to Each Other

I STOOD BEFORE him, his gun trained on me, a willing target.

In the dim moonlight penetrating the kitchen window, I could make out the expansion and contraction of his chest and a sheen on his forehead. He was scared too. He glanced down to the floor and then back to me.

His shoulders slowly relaxed and he let out an exasperated sigh. He lowered the gun. "You're from the project?"

I sighed. "Yes."

"I thought you guys never left that place."

"I'm not supposed to be out."

He chewed on his cheek for a couple of breaths. "If you promise not to tell anyone you saw me, I'll let you go."

"I won't tell anyone. I promise. I'd be in trouble if they found out I left."

His narrowed gaze bore into mine as though trying to burrow into my mind to see if I was telling the truth.

"It's probably a bad idea to trust a Typhon, but . . ." He tucked his gun into his belt. "You're free to go, then."

What if I didn't want to go?

I stepped closer to him, but stopped, my gaze locked on his face. I took in the texture of his skin. One last look at a human. I hadn't realized how much I'd thirsted for the familiarity of human features. Could he be one of the last of his kind?

I forced my feet forward, every step drawing me nearer to him. My heart pounded faster with each stride. I wriggled my fingers. They longed to touch him—even just to graze my fingers over his smooth skin. But I couldn't let them have their way. He would surely recoil from my touch. And it would be weird. I was still human enough to know that.

Before I could pass him, he grabbed my upper arm.

I gasped and stopped short. His warm, soft hand wrapped my arm . . . I was only inches from him. From here, I could see the gold flecks in his brown eyes and, in the middle, perfectly round pupils. I drank in his humanness.

"You shouldn't come back here," he said, and then he let go.

I nodded then hurried through the living room and into the entryway. I slipped my shoes on then opened the door and peered over my shoulder. But he was gone. After stepping outside, I closed the door behind me.

I jogged onto the street and climbed back through the manhole. I sprinted through the cool underground corridor back toward The Farm.

Once there, I threw the hatch open and poked my head out of the hole. The sun was just painting the eastern horizon in oranges and pinks. I climbed onto the perfect lawn inside the dome. I stood, gazed around at my perfect surroundings and my heart sank. I'd returned to my prison.

I ran back to the dorm, sneaked in through the back door, and hopped into my bed. I lay there and stared at the white and textured ceiling.

The Typhon Project

Was the human man even real? Or did I imagine the whole thing?

I rubbed my arm. I could still feel where he grabbed it. He had to be real.

I closed my eyes to force an hour of sleep before I'd have to get up and get ready for class. Images of the human played on my eyelids. I tossed and turned on my bed until doors opened and closed in the hall.

I dragged myself to school. Halfway through first period, exhaustion hit. My eyelids were as heavy as that manhole cover. My third period teacher asked if I was feeling okay. I told her I didn't sleep well.

Though I wanted to take a nap in the worst way, I had work duty at the coil in the afternoon. I was assigned to sweep the floor. Yay for me.

I zoned out, half asleep as I pushed the broom around the massive coil room. The human guy kept popping into my mind, but I forced him out. Maybe I did make him up. Maybe he was a combination of grief, longing, and too little sleep. Who knew.

I jammed the broom into one of the scientist's loafers. He glared at me. I needed to pay closer attention to what I was doing.

Once the big room was clean, I worked my way down the hall—a couple of offices, the break room with the coffee maker. Thoughts of the human gave way to fantasies about my bed. Who was I kidding? I didn't need a bed. Any horizontal surface would do. I checked my watch. Uggh, fifteen more minutes. Would this day never end?

I continued down the hall, farther than I'd ever been. I'd never had a reason to go past the break room. A sign on the door at the end of the hall read RESTRICTED. Hopefully it was locked then I could just be done and hide in the break room amongst the stacks of paper until it was time to go. I twisted the doorknob. Click. Dang. Aren't rooms labeled "restricted" supposed to be locked?

I opened the door. A single computer screen glowed around a silhouette in the dark room. I flipped on the light.

Dean whipped his head to peer back at me, wide-eyed. He blew out a breath. "Leah, it's just you."

"Yeah, just me. What are you doing in here?"

He tapped the keyboard and the screen went black. "I was just . . . looking at something for one of the doctors."

"Looking for something in the dark?"

His eyelids fluttered. "Yeah."

He was lying, but I was too tired to care. I shook my head. "Whatever. I need to sweep in here so I can get out of here. I'm having erotic fantasies about my pillow." I chuckled then slid the broom around the room.

He stood and pushed his hands into his pockets. "Why are you so tired today?" he asked.

I stopped sweeping and leaned on the broom handle. "I'll tell you the truth if you tell me the truth."

His shoulders slumped. "Never mind." He hurried to the door, stuck his head out and glanced side to side then rushed out of the room.

I continued sweeping and about half the floor was clean when the minute hand on my watch hit the twelve. I dumped the broom in the cleaning closet and walked back to the dorm with Dean. He walked with his brow furrowed, staring straight ahead, the only sound between us was our shoes tapping the walkway.

I welcomed the silence. My sleep-deprived brain could no longer form coherent thoughts. When we reached the family room, he strode down the hallway to the guys' rooms, and I went down the girls' hallway.

The Typhon Project

In my room, I dropped onto my bed. One fleeting thought passed through my mind before I fell asleep in my clothes. What was Dean up to in the restricted room?

A song. My morning song. I opened my eyes to dim morning light filtering into the room. My stomach growled and I checked the clock. I'd slept through dinner, straight through until morning.

I pressed snooze and rolled over and savored the feel of my pillow. I let my mind drift and it drifted straight to the human guy. His face was etched in my mind, maybe by fear, though it didn't feel like fear. Where did he come from? And why wasn't he sick? Was he alone or were there other survivors?

Those questions dominated my thoughts as I took a shower and as I dressed and ate breakfast and walked to school with Dean. Zombie this, Zombie that. His voice droned in the background to my booming thoughts.

The human guy probably didn't spend his days in front of a computer playing Zombie Epoch. Or maybe he was healthy because he hid out in a bunker somewhere doing nothing but gaming all the time.

I zoned out in physics.

Did he live in that house or somewhere else? Where did he get food? Were there other humans with him?

". . . torque on a current-carrying coil." My teacher's voice. "Leah, what answer did you get?"

I opened my mouth to answer, but I had no clue what she was talking about. I scanned the board for a clue. My heart sped. I blinked.

"One point four times ten to the negative four Newton meters," Dean whispered behind me.

"One point four times ten to the negative four Newton meters," I said.

The teacher's mouth turned down. "I asked Leah, not you Mr. Green."

I slid down in my chair.

The bell rang and I hurried into the hall.

Dean caught up with me. "What planet are you on today?"

I clutched my books to my chest. "I don't know. My head is somewhere else today. Sorry for getting you in trouble."

"No worries, but now you owe me."

I moaned. "Dean, I don't want to play that game."

"Just watch me play then."

"Fine, but then we're even."

At the door to my next class, my history teacher stopped me. "Dr. Rail would like to see you in her office."

No! "But . . . I don't want to miss your class." Not that I loved history, but I'd take oral surgery over Dr. Rail any day.

"I'll send your work with someone from your family group."

I sighed and stalked off toward my counsellor's office. Was I in trouble for not paying attention in class?

Or—I gasped. Or does she know I sneaked out?

15

The Matchmaker

I WALKED INTO the building that held Dr. Rail's office. I took the stairs to the fifth floor so it would take longer to get there. My feet felt heavier with each step. How would I explain sneaking out? I couldn't say I just got lost. I knew the tunnel was a place I shouldn't have been. Technically though, no one ever said, "Don't go poking around in tunnels."

I strode into the waiting room.

Her assistant peered around her computer screen. "Leah Baines?"

"The one and only." I plopped down in an upholstered chair with oversized arms.

She tapped on her keyboard. "You can go right in, dear."

I sighed and pushed out of the chair. My hand on the doorknob to Dr. Rail's office, I hesitated. I could do this. Just act casual. I twisted the knob and opened the door.

Dr. Rail smiled. "Please. Come in and close the door behind you."

I sat in the chair across from her desk and gripped the wooden arms.

Dr. Rail rested her folded hands on the desk. "Leah, so good to see you again."

I stared at her. She probably expected me to return the pleasantry, but I was in no way happy to see her.

I raised my eyebrows. "You wanted to talk to me?"

"Yes. Two of your teachers have contacted me regarding your performance. They say you're withdrawn, distracted. So, I thought we should have a little chat. How has your transition been going?"

I gripped the chair's arms tighter. "Fine."

"Do you feel like you're fitting in?"

No. "Yeah, sure."

"Have you made friends?"

Maybe one. "Oh yeah. Lots. The people in my family group are great." Whatever she wanted to hear. Whatever got me out of her scaly presence fastest.

She stroked her chin. "An important part of this transition is forming meaningful relationships. While they can't replace those you've lost, over time they can provide the emotional support you need to move forward. Do you feel you've formed meaningful connections?"

I shifted in my chair. "Yeah, I think so."

She tilted her head. "You've become good friends with Dean Green, haven't you?"

I narrowed my eyes. The question seemed loaded. "Yes, we're friends."

She pressed her lips together into a tight smile. She drew a breath, then said, "You might find a relationship an excellent distraction from your grief and a good emotional outlet."

I stiffened. Didn't I just tell her I'd made some meaningful connections? I shook my head. "Okay. Sounds good."

"Leah, you look confused."

"I guess, a little. I just told you I've made some meaningful connections, and now you're telling me I need a relationship."

"Let me clarify. I'm sure you remember the series of tests we gave you when you were first accepted into the program. IQ tests, personality tests."

"I remember."

She stood, walked around to my side of the desk, and leaned against it. She folded her arms and looked down at me. "You and Dean came up as highly compatible, which is why we placed the two of you in a family group together."

My mouth dropped open. Was she seriously suggesting . . . ? "Dean is my friend. Nothing more."

"Why don't you give it a try?" she said as though she was asking me to sample a new soft drink. "An amorous relationship with the opposite sex can be a delightful distraction. Try it out. I'm sure you won't be sorry." She smiled and clapped her hands together. "Now that that's settled you are free to go."

Settled? What was settled?

I walked out of her office. Her assistant bid me goodbye. I didn't respond. I shuffled down the hall to the elevator and pressed the button. Was she seriously trying to set me up with Mr. Zombie Epoch? I stepped onto the elevator. Anger simmered in my chest. What? Did she think she was some sort of matchmaker?

I crossed the courtyard to my dorm. By the time I reached my room, the anger had intensified into a full-on, roiling boil. I dropped onto my bed. Did that really just happen? Dean of all people. Nice guy, but no.

My body's need for sleep trumped my anger. I closed my eyes and drifted.

———————

A knock.

Another knock, louder this time. I opened my eyes. "Come in."

Dean peeked inside. "You ready?"

My stomach clenched. "For what?"

He stepped into my room. "You were going to watch me play. Remember?"

My shoulders relaxed. "Oh yeah, that's right."

"You don't have to." He shrugged. "That's okay."

"No, I said I would. I keep my word."

"I know you do, but I'm going to let you off the hook. I don't even know if I feel like playing tonight."

I laughed. "Wow, that's a sure sign of the apocalypse."

"I know, I know. Just when you think you've got me figured out, I totally amaze you. I do that to people all the time."

I inspected the lines on my hands. Dean was my only real friend here. "What would I do without you, Dean?" I looked him over. Nothing. He felt like a brother, nothing else.

His lips curled up into a playful grin. "Your life would be miserable without me. How about a walk instead?"

"A walk would be good."

We left through the back door and meandered down the sidewalk. "Where are we going?" I asked.

"Everywhere."

"Why so vague all the time?"

"Maybe I don't want to be locked in. If I tell you where we're going, I have to go there. I can't change my mind."

"You're welcome change your mind. It's not like I'll hold it against you."

The Typhon Project

We strode toward the Tesla coil in the dimming light. "How would you like to see the coil without any white coats around to give us a hard time?"

"Are we allowed?"

"Oh yeah, for sure." He smirked. "Especially when they don't know we're going."

"So this is covert?"

He chuckled. "All the way, baby."

"What about the cameras?"

"I'll just tell them I wanted to show you around without getting in the scientists' way. They'll tell us we need to leave and reprimand us. Then we'll say sorry, won't happen again and we'll leave."

"Solid plan."

He pressed his thumb to the box beside the door then opened it and motioned for me to go inside. He followed, then hurried ahead of me to open the steel door. He led me into the huge coil room. Usually a hub of activity, it was strange seeing it without any white coats. The coil's pulsating hum broke the silence and the faint smell of ozone hung in the air.

"Now you can tell me what all this stuff is for," I said.

"That's why we're here."

I followed Dean around the room and, one machine at a time, he explained what each did. I hung on his every word. He opened up one of the laptops and pulled up a window full of data. He pointed at the screen and described all the measurements and what they meant.

I pointed at a column of data on the screen. "What does this mean?"

His gaze fixed on my watch. His brow furrowed, and he grabbed my wrist and brought it closer. "It's pointing north."

I tried pulling my arm back, but he held on. "Yeah, it always does when I'm in here."

He blinked a couple of times and then released my wrist. "That's weird."

"This thing creates a strong magnetic field, I suppose."

He chewed on his cheek. "Want to see something else?" He shoved his hands in his pockets.

"Sure."

I followed him toward another set of instruments, but he turned around. Sweat glistened on his forehead. I waited for him to say something. His gaze darted to the side and then back to me. He stepped toward me. I shuffled backward, but he grabbed my arms. He planted his lips on mine. I struggled to pull away, but he held on. I wound up and kicked his shin. He let out a gasp and then let go. I stumbled backward.

"What the hell, Dean?" I wiped my hand over my lips to wipe off what he left behind.

16

My Only Friend

I SCRUBBED MY fingers over my lips to get every last molecule of Dean's kiss off my lips.

He hopped on one foot. "You kicked me!"

"Yeah, I kicked you. If that didn't work I was going to knee you in the balls. You colossal asshole!"

I spun and darted for the door. I glanced over my shoulder. He limped after me. I shoved the door open, hurried through, then slammed the door in his face.

Tears flooded my eyes. My one friend. My only friend!

The door slammed again behind me. "Leah, wait!"

Tears blurred the path. I wiped them on the back of my hand and broke into jog.

"Leah! Stop. I just want to talk to you. Please!" Dean's feet thumped closer.

I stepped off the sidewalk and took off across the lawn. I glimpsed Dean out of the corner of my eye. He ran toward me. I lengthened my stride and sprinted toward the dormitory. Nearing the door, I slowed and reached for the lever. He smacked into the door and blocked me.

I yanked on the handle. "Move!"

He doubled over, trying to catch his breath. "Just . . . listen."

I folded my arms across my chest and glared at him. "Get out of my way. Now!"

He put his hands up as though in surrender. "I'm sorry. I'm really, really sorry. It was a stupid thing to do. I'm so sorry."

I pressed my lips together and looked away.

He moaned. "Oh, crap. I made you cry, too. I'm an ass, you're right. Kick me again, this time in the balls. I deserve it. Make it a good one. I'll know it's good if I feel a crunch." He stepped sideways to give me a wider target.

He was trying to make me laugh, but I wasn't about to let him cover this with humour. "Shut up, Dean."

"Just let me explain."

"I don't want to hear it. That was a violation, Dean!"

"Please. Pleeeease."

"No!"

He dropped to his knees and folded his hands together. "Please, Leah. You're right. I was wrong to do that. Just give me a chance to explain."

I sighed. "Fine."

"Look, I'm not smooth like other guys. I didn't really know how to do this. I met with my counsellor today and he said . . ."

"Wait, your counsellor put you up to this?"

"Yeah. I mean, no."

"Well, which is it?"

"He suggested it and—well, I can't say I minded the idea or hadn't thought of it before."

I shook my head.

"He said your counsellor was going to talk to you about it, too, so I thought now was a good time. But I guess you weren't feeling the same thing." His shoulders slumped and he looked down. "I guess the friendship thing is probably over now, too?"

"You could have tried asking if I was okay with it!"

"I should have. I'm an idiot. It'll never, never happen again."

I didn't want to lose my only friend, and he seemed sincere. He didn't have a mean bone in his body, but how could I trust him now? And why did his counsellor put him up to this? Were his counsellor and mine conspiring? Weren't counsellors just supposed to listen and help people make decisions, not make decisions for them?

His eyes turned glassy.

"Dean, don't do the puppy dog thing. I still want to be your friend. I just can't be that type of friend, okay?"

"I am truly sorry."

"It's okay. I forgive you, but don't ever, ever do that again. Okay?"

"I won't, but if you ever want to kiss me, you should know that I'm open to that."

I shook my head. "I'll keep that in mind. Is your leg okay?"

He lifted his pant leg. A purple goose egg swelled on his shin. "You got me good."

"Come on, let's go find some ice."

He went to the Tesla family room while I went to the kitchen to scrounge up an ice pack. When I found him later, he had his pants rolled up to the knee and his leg propped up on the coffee table. I tossed him the ice pack.

He flashed me his signature playful smile. "Thanks."

I plopped down on the sofa across from him and hugged a throw pillow to my chest. He winced as he placed the ice pack on his leg. "You know, you're the first girl I ever kissed."

"Really?"

"Yeah.

I felt kind of sad for him that his first kiss turned out the way it did. The first time Graeme kissed me, there was this achy need and then elation. That's the way a first kiss should be—it shouldn't end in the need for an ice pack.

He leaned forward and fidgeted with the corners of the ice pack. "Am I the first guy you've ever . . ."

"No."

"Oh." His smile faltered, but then brightened. "How did I do? Was it a good kiss? I mean, compared with the other guy?"

I sighed. "I'm traumatized." I was glad Dean's kiss wasn't my first; I might never have done it again.

"That good, eh?"

I rolled my eyes. "I'm going to bed."

That night I dreamt about Graeme. Dean's misguided kiss attempt must have brought memories of kissing Graeme to the surface. I missed his kisses and his touch. Would I ever have that again? My only choices here were other Typhons, and I didn't find a single one of them attractive in the least. Not that I could have any sort of relationship with a human—even if they still existed— they'd be repulsed by me.

I considered the human guy but forced him out of my mind. The more time that passed, the more he felt like a figment of my imagination. Maybe the tunnel, the house, and he were all just a vivid dream.

As the days passed, the urge to go back into the tunnel increased. I told myself it was stupid. The guy wouldn't be there anyway. He said he didn't live there. He was probably just searching for food, and I happened to be there. But, what if he was there? But then what? It's not like he would want to be anywhere near a Typhon.

My thoughts chased each other round and round like that all week. One night, I sneaked outside and stood over the door to the shaft but forced myself to go back to my dorm. I would only be disappointed if I went searching for him.

The next night, I lay in my bed staring at the ceiling. The stupid cricket outside my window must have had a megaphone attached to his legs—legs that I'd be happy to pull off one by one right now. The comforter was too hot so I kicked it off the bed. Then I was cold. I pulled the comforter off the floor and punched my pillow. Everything felt so damned uncomfortable.

I knew my bed was not the problem. I wanted to be running down a long cement tunnel toward a house that could have been home. Maybe I'd just go for a little walk to clear my head and then I'd be able to get to sleep.

I slipped out again and, like an addict, I justified every step toward the shaft. Thin self lies drove me across the lawn in the darkness.

I was just taking a walk.

I'd just peek into the shaft.

I could use the exercise, and the tunnel was such a nice place to run.

I threw open the hatch and stared down the hole. My heart raced. A glance around to make sure no one was watching, and then I climbed down the ladder and into the tunnel.

I flicked on the lights and I ran. I knew where I was going this time so concentrated on moving myself forward, faster and faster.

17

The Haunted House

I PUSHED ASIDE the manhole cover and climbed out onto the street. I went straight to the house, my mission so different from last time. Last time, I was hoping to see ghosts; this time I wanted to see flesh and blood.

I stood on the front step, my hand on the door lever. Would he be here? My eyes thirsted to see a human again.

No. I couldn't get my hopes up.

And yet, bright, euphoric expectation filled me as I walked through the door. I listened but the house was silent. I hurried toward the kitchen. I wanted to find him in the same spot where I'd left him. I held my breath as I stepped onto the vinyl floor, but the kitchen was empty.

I searched upstairs, avoiding the baby's room, then searched the basement. Nothing. Emptiness—so empty my insides seemed to drain until they were as empty as the house.

My chest tightened. Of course he wasn't here. Why would he be? It's not like he spent his nights resisting coming back to this house or thinking about why I'd been here.

Why did I come here?

Maybe I just wanted normal, familiar—home.

But I could never go home again. Even if I could, there'd be no Dad or Mom or Lindsay. My house, if it hadn't been reduced to ash by a solar flare, would be as empty as this one. Just a shell that used hold everything important.

I made my way to the living room, laid back on the sofa and draped my legs over the armrest. Tears dripped down my temples. Combing my fingers through my hair, I stared at the ceiling. I closed my eyes and conjured images of my family. The images didn't seem as crisp as they usually were. Was I forgetting? No, no, no! I couldn't let that happen. I concentrated harder and they came in to focus.

And the guy that was here last time? Maybe he wasn't even real. Maybe he was just a symbol for all I'd lost. Maybe I made him up. Maybe he was a ghost. All I have are ghosts.

Especially now, after what happened with Dean. He said sorry, but it felt like there was this bubble between us now. I couldn't trust what was on his mind anymore.

When I first arrived at The Farm, I'd thought maybe I could honour Mom's request to save the world by working on the Tesla coil, but I'm nothing more than a custodian or a barista there. I couldn't save the world by pouring coffee.

I should've been heading back to The Farm, but nothing drew me back. Dr. Rail had been right—I didn't fit in. I couldn't accept what I'd become.

How could I love Dean when I couldn't even look at him?

Maybe I'd never head back. Maybe I'd just live here.

My body relaxed and I drifted.

A voice woke me. "Damn it."

My eyes shot open. A dark figure hovered over me. I gasped.

"What are you doing here?" The voice was familiar. I rubbed my eyes and he came into focus.

His gun hung on his belt this time.

"I said, what are you doing here?" He spoke slower and louder this time.

A smile threatened to break through, but I held it back.

Say something! Don't just stare at him. "I just—I um . . ."

He shook his head. "Didn't I tell you not to come back here?"

I remembered our brief conversation too well. "You said I shouldn't come back here."

He strode to the window, tucked himself against the curtain, and peered out the window as though he were keeping watch. Was he?

"Why are you here?" he asked, his gaze pinned on the street outside.

I bit my lip. I didn't have a good answer for that question. "Why are you here?"

He glanced over his shoulder. "I asked you first."

"Fine. I couldn't sleep so I decided to take a walk. Now you."

He turned back to the window. "I like the view."

I sighed.

He left the window and sat on the sofa across from me. His elbows resting on his knees, he said, "It's hard to tell when a Typhon is lying, but I'm pretty sure you are. Maybe you can answer this one honestly—What's your name?"

The way he said "Typhon" made my stomach twist. It was as though he loathed us. I swallowed hard. "I'm Leah. What's yours?"

"Jace." His gaze narrowed. "Were you here to talk to Lindsay again?" He remembered her name.

"Not this time." I had so many questions for him. "How is it you're not sick?"

He peered down at his hands. "I haven't seen daylight in five years."

"In five years? Where have you been?"

He jumped to his feet. "That's none of your business, Typhon. I shouldn't be here. You're going to run back to your kind and report me to them."

Report? As though he was some sort of criminal? "I won't tell anyone."

A gust of humorless laughter, and then he said, "Yeah, right. Like I can trust a Typhon."

The back of my neck warmed. "I know we look weird, but we all were people like you not long ago."

He lifted his chin. "Not all of you. I take it you're one of those they changed."

"What do you mean not all of us? And, yes, I used to be like you."

"I mean the ones that have always been Typhon."

"No one has always been Typhon."

"Lies. See, you're all liars."

I stood and clenched my hands into fists. "I'm not a liar."

"Whatever you say."

"I'm not lying."

"Why do you keep coming here to talk to your dead sister?"

I squared my shoulders. "I don't know. I miss her. I know it doesn't make sense." I swallowed against the lump in my throat. "And I don't know why I came back here other than this house looks like where I used to live and coming here . . . coming here felt like coming home."

He tilted his head. "I wonder . . ."

"What?"

"Do they know you're here?" he asked.

"No, I sneaked out. I'm sure I'd get in huge trouble if they found out."

His gaze darted to the window then back to me. "Leah, it may be dangerous for you to be here."

"Dangerous? How? I'll go back before sunrise, and besides, my skin can take it."

He furrowed his brow. "You're not in danger from the sun." He brushed his hand over his gun. "You won't tell them you saw me."

I shook my head. "Of course not."

"Because that would be very, very bad for me."

"Why? Are you some sort of . . . criminal?"

"I'm human. That's enough."

"They don't care. Maybe they'd be interested to know that you survived and . . ."

"Interested? Yeah, they'd be interested—so interested that they'd hunt me down and kill me."

"Who?"

He wrinkled his nose. "Who do you think? The Typhons! Feigning ignorance isn't a good look."

"They wouldn't kill you. If they knew there were still humans alive . . ."

He threw up his hands. "If they knew? They know. They're exterminating us before the others get here."

"They wouldn't do that. They're preserving us—the last remnant of humanity for when they get the Tesla coil working, and they can restore the magnetic field."

He smirked. "You don't really believe all that?"

"It's the truth."

"You are brainwashed."

I bristled. "No, I'm not."

"You're telling me they are preserving humanity by destroying it, by changing it into something different? Does that make any sense?"

"It was the only way we could survive until the coil . . ."

He chuckled. "What do you think the coil does?"

"When they get it working it will create an artificial magnetic field."

He pointed up. "Lie number one."

"It's not a lie!"

"We don't need the coil. The field flipped south five years ago, and that coil is counteracting it, cancelling it out."

I lifted my chin. "That's not true. What would be the point?"

"The point is to kill us all off so that they can take over. We've heard from others that ships are already arriving."

"Ships? Like boats?"

He burst out laughing, laughing so hard he doubled over.

I glared at him. "What's so funny?"

"You," he said between fits of laughter. "Boats!" He glanced at the window and stopped laughing. I followed his stare. Dark camouflaged figures marched down the street. A beam of red light penetrated the window. The pinpoint spot of laser light floated along the wall opposite the window and then disappeared.

He dropped to his haunches. "Get down!"

18

The Other Typhons

THE HUMAN SWORE under his breath, then grabbed my arm, and yanked me down. Crouching on the carpet, I asked, "Who are they?"

He furrowed his brow. "As if you don't know. You told them about me. You led them right to me!" He gripped my arm so tight he cut off the circulation.

I attempted to pry his hand away, but he only held on tighter. "I have no idea who they are. I didn't tell anyone about you."

"Liar. I guess it's just a coincidence that soldiers show up here at the same time as you."

"Soldiers?"

"Yeah, Typhon soldiers." He inched his head higher and higher—probably so he could see out the window—then ducked down again.

"Like a Typhon army? No, no, there's no such thing." There were no soldiers at The Farm. I tried again to tug my arm away. "Let go of me."

"Why? So you can give away my location?"

"No, because you're hurting me."

He glanced at my arm and loosened his grip enough that my fingers warmed as the blood flow returned.

He ventured another peak out the window and swore again. "They're coming."

"It's okay. If there are Typhon soldiers, they wouldn't hurt us."

"Maybe not you, but they'll kill me."

"They wouldn't. You're a healthy human. You might be the last one. If anything, they'd protect you."

"They're exterminators, Leah. We have to hide."

He rose to his feet, back hunched, and towed me upstairs. The front door creaked. He led me into the baby's room, opened the slatted closet doors, and pushed me inside. After joining me in the dark, cramped space, he closed the doors. He arranged tiny dresses in front of us.

"You want to convince me that you'll keep me a secret?" he whispered. "Then don't make a sound."

If he was wrong about them, why was I so afraid?

Silence hung around us like the clothes on the rack. My breathing and his breathing were jet engines against it. I listened for an sign of the soldiers, but nothing carried above the sound of my pulse in my ears. Maybe they checked out the house and then left? My tense muscles began to relax.

Then, a groaning sound. Like a squeaky stair.

Footsteps in the hall and then inside the baby's room. Boots brushing carpet. A figure threw a dim shadow under the closet door as it moved by. I squinted to peer through the louvered slats of the door, trying to get a glimpse of the soldier. He took a step closer, bringing him into view. The thing had the shape of a man, but even in the moonlight, I could tell its skin wasn't like mine. It was a deep hue and rough like crocodile skin. He held a huge gun with a laser sight.

My mouth fell open and Jace threw his hand over it, wrapped his other hand around my waist, and pulled me against the back wall of the closet. The soldier paused in front of the closet doors.

Did it hear us? My heart battered my ribs. I held my breath.

It turned and stalked out of the baby's room. Footfalls grew silent.

Jace's mouth to my ear, he whispered, "Quiet. Don't move." A chill rippled down my spine.

His chest against my arm, I could feel his heart beating.

Downstairs the door creaked again. Were they leaving?

A thud. The door closing.

I glanced sideways at Jace, looking for a cue that we could move. He shook his head in small tight motions.

Minutes passed in breaths and heartbeats. How long would we have to stay here? I couldn't stay much longer or I wouldn't make it back to The Farm before sunrise.

Jace lowered his hand from my mouth. He silently pushed the baby clothes out of the way and peered between the slats of the door then looked back at me, his index finger pressed to his lips. "Stay here. I'm going to go see if they're gone." He pulled his gun out of his belt. It looked like a toy compared to the weapon the creature carried.

My anxiety spiked. If he went up against that thing, he'd lose. "What if they're still here?"

"I know what I'm doing. Stay here and don't move."

I grabbed his arm. "If they're hunting you, I should go. They won't hurt another Typhon." Though they'd likely report that I sneaked out.

He slid open the closet door—just a crack—and peered through. "Why, so you can tell your buddies where I am?"

"I don't know who or what they are, but they're not my buddies. And if I would've wanted them to catch you, I could've done that when that soldier was in here."

His eyes narrowed, seeming to consider my words. "Maybe. But I'm not taking the chance. Stay here and don't make a sound."

He opened the door just enough to squeeze his body through. He darted to the wall beside the door and flattened himself against it. He cranked his head to get a glimpse of the hallway and then raised his gun and disappeared into the hall.

I strained my ears against my raging pulse to listen for any sign of trouble. Would I know if the creature found him, or would he simply not come back? I leaned my head back against the closet wall and breathed through my anxiety.

I checked my watch. How long had he been gone?

More footsteps, these lighter than the creature's. Jace rounded the doorway into the bedroom and tucked his gun back in his belt. "All clear. They're gone."

What if they were hiding somewhere and lying in wait for us? "You sure?"

"Yeah, you can come out." He extended his hand to me.

I stepped out of the closet. "What was that thing?"

"I told you. A soldier. A Typhon."

The color and texture of its skin—it didn't look like any Typhon I'd ever seen. It looked more reptilian than anyone at The Farm. More animal than human. And yet, Jace saw that creature and me as one and the same.

My stomach dropped. That creature and I weren't the same, were we? But we were. The same species. I wanted to be more like Jace, but in truth, I was just as much the animal as that soldier.

A Typhon like me. That razor cut at me again. That creature was like me, and I was like him. The same species.

Jace waved me forward. "Come on."

A lump formed in my throat and tears stung at my eyes. Self-hatred washed over me, powerful and staggering, like a tsunami. I lifted my hands and looked at the fine silver scales that covered my fingers. I balled them into fists and watched the scales pivot past each other.

"Don't be scared. It's gone," he said.

It.

He called the Typhon "it." I'm an "it." My stomach lurched

"What's wrong?" he asked.

When he looked at me, did he see that thing? Was that what I was to human eyes?

The air thinned. All these months of avoiding the mirrors and cringing at the sight of Dr. Rail and the other students crashed in on me.

"I'm a Typhon. Like him." I bit my cheek and blinked away the tears. "Do I—Is that what I look like to you?"

He blinked a couple times. "Um." His gaze moved over me.

Why did I ask that question? We were hiding from soldiers who he claimed wanted him dead, and I was concerned I didn't look good. "Never mind," I said.

"You don't . . ."

I put my hand up to stop him. I had to face facts. I was no longer human. I was a different species than Jace and there was nothing I could do to change that.

He shifted from one foot to the other. "Didn't you all compete to be like this?" He waved his hand over me. "I mean, this is what you wanted, wasn't it?"

I skimmed my fingers over my cheek. "I was competing to survive, not to be like—this. I never wanted this."

"You're not like that soldier—you don't really look like him."

"But I'm the same."

He scratched the back of his head and glanced at the door.

"Forget it." I squared my shoulders. "But I hope you know that I'm not in league with them. I'll keep my promise. No one will ever know about you."

"I'm starting to believe that. But why would you protect me?"

"Because—I don't know—you're human. Maybe the last one."

"Leah, you need to go back where you came from. It's not safe here. And you shouldn't—you can't come back here. Ever."

"I don't want to go back that place."

"It's perfect there, isn't it? Plenty of food, greenery, a safe place to sleep. You don't have to be on the run and watching your back all the time." He roughly ran his hand through his hair, making the hair stand up. "Besides, if you keep coming back, you'll end up getting caught and who knows what they'll do to you." He lifted my wrist and looked at my watch. "Not long until sunrise."

I glanced at my watch. He was right. If I didn't leave now, I risked getting caught. The thought of returning made my shoulders slump, but maybe if I went back, I could find more information about the coil and see if he was right about the coil counteracting the magnetic field or if it all was some paranoid conspiracy theory.

"I guess I should go," I said.

He sighed. "Yeah, me, too."

Neither of us moved for a couple long moments.

I huffed out a breath. "Goodbye, Jace." I took a step toward the door.

"Uh, yeah. Bye."

I walked into the hall.

"Don't forget your promise," he called after me.

I glanced over my shoulder. "Never."

19

A Crazy Conspiracy

I CLIMBED BACK down the shaft and into the tunnel. Would I make it back in time? I broke into a sprint back toward The Farm.

When I emerged from the shaft back inside the dome; the sun was peeking over the horizon. If only I had the cover of darkness to conceal my journey back to the dorm. I hurried to the path and sped to a run. If anyone saw me, hopefully they'd think I was out for a morning workout.

Even though I'd never rolled out of bed early enough to do that. Well, there was a first time for everything. At least, that's what I'd tell them.

I checked my watch when I was safely inside the dorm. No sense in going to bed—my alarm would wake me in a half-hour and that much sleep would make me more groggy than rested.

I went straight to the shower. I took my time washing and then, closing my eyes, I stood under the stream of hot water and let it pour over me. My mind drifted back down the tunnel to those creatures and to Jace.

And then grief poured over me, soaking me with its hopelessness. He told me never to go back there. My arms went slack at my sides at the idea of never returning there, but a question—a curiosity—drove out the grief.

Who were those soldiers and why were they there? In fact, why were soldiers necessary at all? I mean, everyone is dead except for the few who got transformed into Typhon's like me, and we're all locked in project domes like The Farm. The only reason for soldiers is conflict or threat. And why the guns?

The soldiers seemed to be searching for something. Was Jace right? Were they searching for him or was he just paranoid? They were clearly searching for something. Maybe they were looking for children who were left after their parents died. Like that baby in that room. Maybe the soldiers found the baby and gave it to someone who could care for it until it passed.

Plausible. But the guns. Camouflage and laser sights weren't necessary for rescuing children.

What if Jace was right? What if they were searching for the few humans that survived? What if he was right about all of it?

I turned off the water and dried off. Wrapped in a towel, I walked toward the bathroom door, past the sinks and, over them, the mirrors. Out of habit, I averted my eyes. And then I stopped. Did I look like the soldiers, like those creatures? Was I deluding myself into believing I wasn't as hideous as them? I forced my gaze to the mirror and stepped closer. Then another step. And another. I let my towel drop.

My eyes were shaped like my human eyes, but the pupil was a black slit. I closed my eyes and opened them again. This was me now. I needed to get used to it because there was no going back.

My gaze followed the curve of my shoulders. The silver in my skin caught the light at the bend of my shoulders. My arms were stronger looking than I remembered them, my biceps outlined beneath my shimmering skin. Then I noticed the curve of my breasts and the skin of my stomach stretched between my hips. The soft arc of my hips. It was all the way I remembered it. For the most part, it was my shape. The main difference was that I looked like I'd been dipped in mercury and of course, my skin texture was different.

Not so different from the human me.

Not so different at all. Why did it seem like there were so many differences before?

Maybe I was telling myself what I wanted to hear, but I didn't think I looked like anything like those soldiers.

I picked up my towel, wrapped it back around me, and strode to my room. I dressed and then opened my computer. I clicked on the Tynet icon and then punched Dad's name into the search box: Jordan Baines.

Apparently, there'd been more than a few Jordan Baineses in the world. I narrowed the search by adding the terms, "Air Force" and "plane crash."

The results listed some articles about the accident, and I found his obituary. I read the articles and the obituary, but they didn't reveal anything I hadn't already known—his plane went down over the Persian Gulf while on a routine patrol. Cause unknown.

I punched a couple new terms into the search engine—"Tesla Coil" and then "magnetic field," but neither divulged anything new. I slammed the laptop closed. If they had something to hide, they wouldn't put it on Tynet for students to find. I rested my elbows on the desk and buried my face in my hands. They? They who?

Jace had said they were coming in ships. "Ships?" I said. Ships, but clearly not boats. I sighed. Airships? Spaceships? I chuckled. I'd heard this conspiracy theory once that lizard people from space were taking over the world. Ridiculous. Science fiction. Typhons were changed humans, adapted to survive in the new system. Nothing more.

And then an idea popped into my head, horrible and brilliant at the same time. The sign on the door in the Tesla coil building flashed in my thoughts. Of course, they wouldn't have the information I wanted where students could access it, but perhaps they'd have it on computers that were restricted.

Doors opened and closed in the hall. The others were waking up. Would anyone be in the Tesla building this time of morning? If I got caught, it would certainly arouse less suspicion going there now than it would in the middle of the night. I checked my watch. I had an hour until class started.

I slipped out the back door and walked toward the Tesla building as though I was on a scenic morning stroll. I stopped for a moment to look at the roses, which also gave me a moment to look around to see if anyone was out. A couple of students jogged toward the center of the compound, while another sat under a tree with a black book open across his lap.

I continued walking, formulating excuses for why I would be at the coil so early if I got caught. I decided to go with saying that I'd lost my sweater and thought maybe I left it in the building after my last work duty. The excuse gave me an out when inevitably it wasn't there. Oh well, I must have left it somewhere else.

My heart sped as I approached the coil. A few steps from door, it swung open. I jumped out of the way. Dean strode through the door. His gaze found me and he froze. We stood and stared at each other for a moment.

He formed a tense smile. "Oh, Leah, hi."

"Hi, Dean. Um . . . what are you doing here?"

"Oh, I was . . . uh, behind on some work from . . . you know, last week. So I went to finish it." He rubbed the back of his neck.

"What work would that be? Tweaking Green's Theory of Fluid Dynamics? Grinding coffee?" I smirked.

"Ha, ha, ha. You're so funny. So, what are you doing here?"

I shrugged. "I was just looking for my sweater. Thought maybe I left it here. But now I remember. It's in the laundry. I guess I'll head back."

"Sounds good. I'll join you."

"Perfect."

I ground my teeth. Great. I'd have to find a different time to snoop.

We started down the path back toward the dorm. I glanced over my shoulder at the door to the coil—and possibly the information I needed—growing farther away with each step.

Dean and I walked side by side. His hand brushed mine a couple of times so I moved to the far edge of the sidewalk. He sighed and then stared at the flower beds as we strolled by. Awkward tension buzzed between us. I wanted it to be light and easy like it used to be between us. I wanted my friend back. Key word: friend.

I wanted us to talk. I didn't care about the subject. "You're up bright and early."

"Yeah, you too."

Silence.

"So, um, you find any weeds yet?" I asked.

I took two steps before I realized he'd stopped. I turned back toward him. He tilted his head and said, "I think I have." The sheer seriousness of his expression triggered a chill.

Was he that serious about a weed—or did he mean something else? "Really? A weed? where?"

He swallowed hard. "Everywhere."

"What do you mean?"

He looked back at the coil, then shook his head. "Never mind." He smiled, but it wasn't a true Dean smile. It was cold and forced.

I didn't ask any more questions. Silently, we returned to the dorm. I grabbed my backpack from my room and then headed to class.

I fell asleep in Calculus. Dean shook me awake at the end of class. According to Dean, the teacher had thrown his white board eraser at me. I'd slept through it. He wanted to know why I was so tired lately. I gave him the same excuse as before: hard time sleeping.

I went to my room after school, climbed into bed, and slept like the dead. I overslept the next morning and missed my chance to go to the coil building. At the end of my last class of the day, I got called down to the office. The secretary informed me I had an appointment with Dr. Rail after school. Great.

I stalked through the courtyard, stopping to look at the fish to prolong my walk. I liked the idea of making her wait. A bright orange koi glided through the water, its scales looked beautiful against the dark stone bottom of the pond. I leaned over and dipped my hand in the water. My skin shimmered as the sun caught it.

When I arrived at Dr. Rail's office the secretary told me I could go straight in. I opened the door. Dr. Rail sat at her desk, hunched over and writing something. She didn't acknowledge my presence. I planted myself in one of the chairs in front of her desk and glanced at the clock. Five minutes passed and she was still writing. Then ten minutes went by. I shifted in my seat. Why had she called me here if she didn't have time for me?

I waited another five minutes and then I stood to leave.

Her gaze finally lifted. "Sit down." She pointed at the chair then continued to write. Another five minutes crawled past.

Finally, she dropped her pen. "How were the fish?"

Ah, that's what this was about. She was making me wait because I made her wait.

I glared. "Fine."

"Of course they are. Everything is always fine with you, Leah." She looked me straight in the eye. I squirmed in my seat and looked away.

"Your teachers have informed me that you are sleeping in class again and neglecting your homework," she said.

I shrugged. "Yeah, I didn't sleep well a couple of nights ago. I'm fine now, though."

"Leah, are you happy here?"

"Yeah, it's good."

"Do you miss your home, your family?"

"Yeah, sometimes." More like all the time, but I didn't feel like going into it.

"How are things going with Dean?"

"Fine."

She leaned back in her chair. "Ahh, there's that word again. Honestly, Leah, I'm losing patience with you. I was really hoping I would see some progress by now. Did you take my advice about starting a sexual relationship with Dean?"

"Sexual relationship? Dean? No!"

"You agreed to give it a try last time." She pressed her lips together into a tight line.

I shook my head. "No, I didn't. I didn't agree to that. I thought you meant a boyfriend, girlfriend thing. I'm totally not into Dean that way."

"But the two of you are a perfect match. Both personality wise and genetically." She lifted her chin. "You will start a relationship with him."

20

The Hospital

I COULDN'T BELIEVE what I was hearing. Was she seriously trying to force me into a relationship with Dean? My stomach sank. Something was very wrong here. "The hell I will!"

She eyed me for a long moment. Her eyelids fluttered. "I think I've been going about this all wrong. Maybe this is simply the wrong setting for you. Perhaps you'd open up better elsewhere." She stood and buttoned her blazer. "Leah, let's take a walk."

I gripped the arms of my chair. "I have homework I need to work on."

She waved her hand dismissively. "Ah, it's never bothered you to ignore it before." She lifted her chin and her eyes narrowed. "Now."

A shiver rippled over me. Something in her hardened expression forced me to my feet. She rounded her desk, came alongside me, and threaded her arm through mine. "I have something I want you to see." She grinned. I tried wiggling my arm out of hers, but she held tight.

She escorted me out of the office building, through the courtyard, and toward a building I had never visited before.

"The hospital? Why are we going to the hospital?" I said.

She smiled. "You'll see." And then she leaned closer and whispered in my ear, "It's a surprise."

I shuddered.

We strolled through the hospital's entryway and to the elevator. Dr. Rail pressed the up button. I wrinkled my nose at smell of bleach and stale air as I watched the red, glowing numbers counting down floors.

I tried to pull my arm away again, but she didn't release me. My pulse throbbed in my ears. Why were we here? What could she need to show me in a hospital? My frantic imagination couldn't even find the answer.

The elevator door slid open and she marched me inside. She pressed the button for the sixth floor. The door closed.

She squeezed my arm tighter. "Last night you were trying to access some information on Tynet. Information about your father and the magnetic field and the coil. What were you looking for?"

"You were tracking me online?"

"It's our network and our computer. We do what we want. What were you looking for?"

The elevator stopped and the doors opened. A wide hall with mint green walls spread out in front of us.

My heart pounded so hard against my ribs that I thought it might break through. My gut told me it was a bad idea to get off the elevator. Dr. Rail stepped forward, but I didn't budge.

She looked at me, her eyes blank, emotionless. "Come along, Leah."

"No," I whispered.

She pressed her free arm against the door to keep it from closing. "Guard."

A figure stepped into view: One of the crocodilian creatures I'd seen at the house. I gasped and stumbled backward.

Dr. Rail yanked me forward. "You can come on your own or he can force you."

I stared at him—even more hideous than the others had been in the darkness at the house. I swallowed hard and stepped forward.

"That's a good girl." She nodded at the creature. "Stand down."

The creature stepped aside.

She walked me down the hall, my shoes squeaking against the shiny industrial tiles. "Leah, someone has been accessing information on the restricted computers—the same information you were searching for on Tynet last night. Do you know anything about that?"

Dean. Dean was on the restricted computers . . . and he was looking up the same information as I was? "I don't. I was just looking up stuff about my dad. There's nothing wrong with that."

"Nope, nothing at all. But I doubt it's a coincidence that you just happened to be looking up the same information as whoever has been hacking into the restricted computers. And it just so happens you work inside the coil."

"I've never been on the restricted computers. I swear I haven't."

She laughed. "Of course not."

We stopped in front of a set of double doors at the end of the hall. Dr. Rail took a card from her breast pocket and swiped it over a sensor beside the door. A buzz rang out and she thrust the door open. She pushed me through it. A plaque on the wall read, PSYCHIATRIC WARD.

21

Lesson Learned

THE HEAVY DOOR to the psychiatric ward closed behind me, and my legs went numb. Dr. Rail seized my arm and dragged me forward. "You haven't adapted well, Leah. You've not met our expectations."

She towed me into a broad room. Bars striped the large windows. Patients wrapped in light yellow bathrobes sat motionless in chairs around a small TV, their backs to me.

Dr. Rail yanked my arm and walked me around to the front of the half circle of patients. They didn't seem to notice our presence. Their eyes were blank, distant. Some stared at the floor, others toward the TV, but not at it.

Dr. Rail took a deep breath and smiled. "Leah, I'd like to introduce you to some of our patients. She put her hand on the shoulder of the first girl in the circle; the girl didn't register the touch. "This is Abigail and she was so unsettled about her appearance that she tried to remove her skin with a pair of scissors. Can you believe she preferred her weak pink skin to our superior Typhon skin?"

She glanced at me and then back to the patients. "And that is Daniel." She pointed to a boy in the middle. "Daniel tried to escape from The Farm, clearly an act of insanity. Why would anyone in their right mind want to leave someplace so perfect?" She shook her head.

I peered down at the floor; I couldn't bear to look at their vacant eyes any longer.

"Don't look away, Leah, I have one more person I'd like you to meet."

I swallowed hard and lifted my gaze.

"And the red-haired boy is Robert," Dr. Rail said. "He got this idea in his head that we just couldn't talk him out of. He was raving about an alien invasion." She laughed.

Robert's red-haired wig was eschewed. Why did they even bother with it?

"And that chair," Dr. Rail pointed to an empty chair on the other side of the semi-circle, "is for you."

My chest constricted, and I tried to breathe but couldn't. I shook my head. "No, no! Please." I attempted pulling my arm away from her grip but she dug her fingernails into my skin. She waved her free hand, motioning to someone behind me. I cranked my neck. A nurse marched toward me with a syringe.

Tears flooded my eyes. "I can do better. Please! I'll do what you want."

"I don't know, Leah. You've been so rebellious—not paying attention in class, refusing to start a relationship with Mr. Green, going into places you don't belong. You're generally uncooperative."

"I'll cooperate." My breathing came hard and fast. "I will."

She lifted her hand and the nurse stopped. She stroked her chin and scrutinized me. "You seem like you mean it."

"I do. I promise to do better. I've just had a . . . a hard time with all the changes, but it's getting better. I think I'm over it now."

She squared her shoulders. "Your aptitudes are of interest to us, especially in offspring, so we would prefer your mind and body not to rot in here. It would be such a waste. But I do have conditions, and I expect them to be met."

A scream echoed down the hall.

I nodded. "Whatever you want."

She flashed a wide, satisfied smile. "See, I knew a change of scenery would help your attitude. So here is what I want. I need you to engage in your classes and do your homework. No more falling asleep in class. And you will begin a relationship with Dean Green. Do you understand?"

I nodded.

"Do you understand?" She raised her voice.

"Yes."

"And there will be no more snooping around on computers."

I stared at the red-haired boy—Robert—who had the same delusion as Jace. "Okay." Was it a delusion?

"Do you think you can manage that."

"I can. I know I can."

"Well, then, our business here is done. Goodbye all." She waved at the catatonic patients.

This time I didn't resist as she directed me down the hall. In fact, I wanted to run away from this place. We walked past the crocodilian guard then stepped onto the elevator. I glanced over at her. "Didn't you have a hard time adjusting when you were first changed? I mean, doesn't everyone?"

She chuckled and then broke out in laughter. "I had no such adjustment. I was born this way. Of course, you'll find yourself back on the sixth floor if you tell anyone that. Isn't this nice that we can share all of our secrets now?"

Born this way? My mind raced. She'd never been human. Jace was right. There'd been an invasion and no one knew about it. My stomach churned. I swallowed the bile creeping up my throat.

She smiled again and then the elevator doors opened.

"Why are you doing this? Why not just kill us all?" I asked.

She faced me in the wide hospital entryway. "Do you enjoy history? No, of course you don't. You sleep through history. I've learned that if you want to predict the future, simply look to the patterns of the past. And good ideas are good ideas no matter what species you are."

She continued. "Lately, I've been studying your human history books and some of your religious writings. What we're doing is really a very old idea. According to the book of Daniel, the Israelites were defeated by the nation of Babylon. Just like humans have been defeated by Typhons. This Babylonian king had the right idea and I quote, '. . . bring in some of the Israelites from the royal family and the nobility—young men without any physical defect, handsome, showing aptitude for every kind of learning, well informed, quick to understand, and qualified to serve in the king's palace.'"

Dr. Rail patted my cheek. "We are using the best of humanity to make us stronger."

We walked into the courtyard. She smoothed her blazer. "Now, Leah, see to it that you follow our rules. We'll be watching." With that she marched, heels hammering against the cement, back toward her office. I stood, trembling on the sidewalk, watching her go.

I meandered down the sidewalk. My legs jittered and threatened to give out with every step. Serve. They've made us like them to serve them. We competed—I competed for the privilege of allowing them to take my humanity from me. I held out my hands in front of me and splayed by fingers. My breathing hitched. I veered off the path and leaned against a tree for support.

This skin. I hated this skin. I wanted to rip it off. Like Abigail with the scissors. I understood her now.

I peered up into the tree's foliage. Dr. Rail said they'll be watching. They could have cameras anywhere and everywhere. I forced my legs to move. I had to do what they asked. I had to pull it together.

I somehow made it back to the dorm. Inside, I hurried down the hall to the Faraday family room. I stopped in the doorway. Parminder sat in an easy chair reading. Drake lightly snored on the sofa.

If only I could go to my room, lock the door, and dissolve into a teary heap. But if I did that, I may not ever come out. I needed to do this while I was numb, before everything sank in and I fell apart. I had to start a relationship with Dean.

My life depended on it.

22

Getting to Know Dean

Swallowing back tears, I shuffled down the hallway to the boys' rooms. Which room was Dean's? Some of the doors were open, some were closed. I was not in the mental state to go door to door and make apologies when I got the wrong one.

I pressed my eyes closed then opened them again. Memories of the psychiatric ward flashed through my mind. I had to do this. I couldn't end up catatonic, imprisoned in my own head. I had to do this. "Dean!" I shouted. "Dean, where are you?"

I waited, watching all the doors. He poked his head out of the third door on the left. "Hey, Leah. Whatcha doing?"

I took a few steps closer. "I need to talk to you."

"Sure, come on in."

He opened the door wider and motioned me in. I had to step over clothes strewn over the floor to get more than two steps inside. His zombie game was paused on a large screen that took up most of the wall opposite his bed, blankets twisted into a pile. It smelled like boy—feet and armpit. Muted voices crawled from a set of headphones resting at the foot of the bed.

Dean dropped onto his mattress and picked up his controller again. "What's up?"

Books sat in small piles on every surface. The walls were plastered with posters: one of Einstein with a wide, curling handle-bar moustache drawn on it in purple marker, one showed characters from Star Wars jamming in a rock band together, and another had a black and white kitten on it with the phrase, "Every time someone calls tech support, a kitten dies."

I stared at Einstein. He knowingly stared back. Was he smirking? I can't do this in here.

"Sorry for the mess, if I knew you were coming . . ." Dean scratched the back of his head.

I skimmed my teeth over my bottom lip. "That's okay. Don't worry about it."

He fidgeted with the buttons on the controller. "Are you okay?"

I nodded and then sat down on the bed beside him.

"So . . . what did you want to talk about?" he asked.

My throat dried. I swallowed to wet it. "Um, I thought maybe you'd show me how to play that game."

"Really?" He placed his hand to my forehead. "You don't feel feverish."

I wanted to sound more convincing. "No, I'm serious."

His brow furrowed. "You look kind of sick."

"I'm not. Just tired."

The creases between his eyebrows deepened, and he blinked a couple of times before he got up and went to his dresser. He dug around for a moment, then pulled out another controller. He returned to the bed and handed it to me.

He described what each button did. My cloudy mind couldn't focus. Everything he said seemed like a foreign language. I didn't want the clouds to clear. Maybe what I had to do wouldn't seem real when it was over.

"Make sense?" he asked.

"Not really."

"Okay, well, you can watch me play and when you feel ready to start, let me know."

I nodded. I watched his character stalk through the ruins of a city and slay zombies with axes and machetes, blood splashing over the screen. Once he got them all, he moved on to a new level.

His character dropped into a scene, different from the one in the previous level. This scene was a modern city in perfect condition—brick buildings with ivy growing up the side, wide colourful flower beds. His first target moved toward him. The creature had scaly, muddy green skin with yellow eyes. It wasn't a zombie at all—it was one of those soldier creatures.

I dropped the controller and it tumbled to the floor. Dean hit pause and looked at me.

I sprang to my feet. "Dean, when you're done here, do you think you could come to my room so we can talk?"

"Yeah, sure. Just let me finish this level."

I walked to my room, went inside and sat on the bed, leaving the door open. I stared straight ahead. My mind was empty; that's the way I wanted it. An image of Jace popped into my head. He was right. Those paranoid ideas he had weren't paranoid at all, which means he was probably right about everything. Those soldiers were trying to kill what was left of humanity. No wonder he didn't trust me. I've become an enemy to my own people.

My heart rate climbed. On the verge of panic, I slowly breathed in and out, trying to calm myself. One wrong move and Dr. Rail would take me to the hospital.

I focused on the wood grain on my dresser until a tapping sound echoed from the door. Dean stood in the doorway. "Hey, you had something you wanted to talk about?"

"Yeah, come on in. And could you close the door?"

"Sure." He swung the door closed and then leaned against my desk. "So, what's up?"

I had cleared my mind too much. The words I needed refused to come and it was pretty much impossible for me to sound alluring at this point. "Can you sit next to me?" I patted the spot on the bed beside me.

"Okay?" His voice pitched higher at the end. He hesitated, then sat down next to me.

I pressed my eyes closed. Now what?

"Leah, what's going on with you?"

I opened my eyes. Dean was my friend. At least I had that. Zero attraction, but he was a nice guy. "Dean . . . I . . ." I touched the collar of his shirt.

His eyes narrowed. "Leah?"

I grabbed a handful of fabric, pulled him toward me and pressed my lips against his. I placed my other hand on his chest. He tensed but quickly relaxed. My stomach churned, but I kept kissing him. I laid back onto my bed and pulled him down with me. His hand moved over my side and around to my back.

I was dying inside. The longer I kissed him, the more of me wasted away. Knowing that I'd have to be naked with him and all the ways he'd be touching me sent a shock of panic through me. I wanted to push him away. No, I have to do this. I slid my hand under his shirt to encourage him further. Tears overflowed my eyes.

His hand brushed my cheek and I felt him pause. He pulled away and scrutinized my face.

"Don't stop." I yanked him back toward me. I needed him to carry this; I needed him to push it forward because I couldn't.

He shook his head and moved farther from me. "Leah, no."

"Dean, please." A sob escaped my throat. "Please." I tugged on his shirt.

His face fell, all humour and playfulness gone. He glanced at the mirror above my dresser and then back at me. He let me pull him down. He lay on the bed next to me, peered into my eyes and kissed me. He grabbed my leg and hitched it over his thigh. His lips moved to my neck and worked their way up to my ear. I felt his breath on my ear.

"You know the truth, don't you?" he whispered.

My breath caught. I pulled away and looked into his eyes. I nodded.

He kissed my lips again and then slid his hand under my shirt, up my back. Then his lips returned to my ear. "They threatened you?"

I nodded again.

Another kiss and then his lips moved back to my ear. "I'm not going to make you do this. Play along, okay?"

"Okay," I mouthed.

He stood and pulled me off the bed. He yanked the comforter open and then he returned to me. He peeled his shirt off and then I let him do the same to me. He tossed my shirt on the floor on the other side of the bed. He got into my bed, guided me in next to him, and then fixed the comforter over our heads.

"Okay, what do you know?" he whispered.

"I know they were never human. I also know that the Tesla coil works. Whenever I'm near it my compass points north, but when the power went off it pointed south. The magnetic field is fine. They're cancelling it out. Apparently, their ships have been landing."

"How do you know that?"

I bit my lip. "I found a way out. I've been on the outside."

"I really wish you would have played Zombie Epoch with me."

I wanted to slap him. How could he go to something as frivolous as that at a time like this? "Dean, this isn't the time."

"It's not what you think it is. We're using the game to strategize against them; the Typhons think we're communicating about the game."

"That's why you were on the restricted computers. You have to stop. They know someone has been on them. They blamed me, but I knew it was you."

"Did you tell—"

"No, of course not."

He released a relieved sigh. "Thank you. I had no idea. Oh, I forgot," he whispered. "We have a part to play." He spoke louder. "Oh, Leah, you're amazing."

"Oh, Dean," I called back.

"You have to sound like you mean it," he whispered.

"Sorry. Dean, I need to get out of here. I need get to the tunnel that runs under the Tesla building."

"There's a tunnel? They're going to be watching you close. You'll have to avoid the cameras." He loudly announced, "Help me with your bra."

I was confused for a moment and then remembered my part.

"There you go, Dean. Yeah right there, that's good."

"That's better," he whispered.

"I don't really have to take my bra off, do I?"

"You don't have to, but you can if you want."

"Dean."

"Just kidding."

"Do you know where the cameras are?" I asked.

"I know exactly where they are. First of all, there's one in your mirror. When we're done here, I'll throw my shirt over the mirror. Once they've seen you've done your duty, they won't be very interested in watching us sleep. It shouldn't arouse any suspicion. You'll have to climb out the window because there are cameras in the hall. Where exactly do you need to go?"

"Near the fence between the dorm and the Tesla building, there's a shaft that leads into a tunnel."

"Perfect. Once you're out go directly to the fence and follow it. There aren't any cameras near the fence. They're all attached to buildings." He smiled. "Now we need to finish off our friends with benefits act. Make me sound good, okay?"

"Oh, oh, oh, Dean," I cried out.

He looked dissatisfied with my performance. "Dean, you're amazing? Dean, you rock my world?" he whispered.

I rolled my eyes. "Oh, Dean, I've never seen anything so big. Yes, right there. Yes, yes, yes!"

"Better," he mouthed.

He pulled the comforter down so we could breathe, and he made a show of kissing me again—except I could tell it was more than a show for him. I wrapped my arms around him and gave him a real kiss. "Thank you," I whispered.

He put his lips to my ear. "It's not easy lying in bed with you like this. You better get going before I decide it needs to happen for real. My willpower is stretched about as far as it will go before it snaps."

He reached down to the floor, grabbed his T-shirt and threw it at the mirror. The shirt hooked over the rosette at the top.

"Yes! First try," he whispered.

I jumped out of bed, found my shirt, and pulled it over my head. I went to the window and opened it just enough for me to squeeze through, but then I turned back. I went to Dean and kissed him again. "Goodbye."

"Don't come back, okay?"

"Okay." Why are boys always saying that to me? I'm afraid I'm going to have to disappoint Jace, that is, if I can find him. If I could tell the survivors what the Tesla Coil does, maybe there's something they could do to stop it.

I climbed out the window and flattened myself against the brick wall. Now to get to the shaft without getting caught.

23

Finding Jace

OUTSIDE THE DORMITORY, I pressed my back against the wall and scanned the eaves and surrounding buildings for cameras. Where they were? I had no idea. All I could do is run for the fence as fast as I could and hope for the best. I planned a route, staying off the paths and skirting the circles of light cast by the pathway lamps.

After hauling in a deep breath, I sprinted toward the fence. I pushed my legs faster and faster, any moment expecting a Typhon soldier to leap from the shadows. The dew on the grass wetted my shoes as my feet thumped over the lawn. The fence loomed ahead. A silvery net in the moonlight. Almost there!

My heart thudded and my pulse raged. I glanced over my shoulder to see if I was being followed.

No one.

I reached the fence, turned right and dashed toward the Tesla Coil. As I pumped my arms, Dad's watch reflected the moonlight. My thoughts raced, tumbling over one another like puzzle pieces flying together of their own accord. Dad. Images glowed in my thoughts— Mom and I in the bunker that last time. She'd said he wanted me to have his watch and that he put it in the mail, addressed to me, the day before he died.

Then, the tiny piece of paper inside—the drawing of the compass with the needle pointing south. Dad knew.

Dad knew the magnetic field had flipped, which meant he had to have known that someone was tampering with it to cancel it out.

Was his plane crash truly an accident? Or had he discovered the alien invasion? Is that why he sent me his watch? To warn me?

A moment of searching and I found the hatch, peeled it open, and descended into the darkness below.

———

Every stride inside the tunnel carried me farther from The Farm. Anger swelled at the name. It was a farm. They were farming former humans, humans they'd sullied with their alien DNA.

Tunnel lights flashed past me. I lengthened my stride. I needed to get to the house and find Jace. But what were the chances he'd be there again? And what would I do if he wasn't there? I had no idea.

When I reached the ladder leading up to the neighborhood, I slowly climbed to street level. I had to be careful. Typhon soldiers could be on the prowl. I lifted the manhole cover just enough to peek out at the street. I searched for any sign of movement. The street seemed empty, but anything could be hiding in the shadows. I watched and listened. The wind whistled against window screens. My heart thudded as I waited. I'd just have to make a run for it.

I lifted the manhole cover higher and eyed the house I'd visited before on the right. About to slide the heavy lid completely aside, movement on my left caught my attention.

A Typhon soldier marched from the side of one of the houses, his rifle strap slung over his shoulder. He stepped onto the house's front walk and his boots thumped on the pavement. I lowered the manhole cover within a centimeter of being closed, just open enough for me to keep an eye on those huge, heavy boots. They walked down the street a couple of houses, then circled around the back and disappeared.

Was he the only one here or were there others?

Minutes of wind whooshing and my pulse racing passed. Finally, the boots reappeared and made their way farther down the street. A few more houses down, he turned down another front walk. I readied myself.

As he vanished into the darkness beside the house, I lifted the manhole cover and climbed out, then eased it closed—slowly, carefully, silently. Then I ran for the familiar house. In the street, I was exposed. I waited for shouts or gunshots. At the side of the house, I threw myself into the shadows and pressed myself against the siding. I peered around the side and watched the house where I'd last seen the Typhon Soldier. Within seconds he emerged.

I waited for him to find the next house to inspect, then I hurried for the door. Depressing the lever, the door clicked open. I stepped inside and closed the door behind me. My breathing coming in gasps, I slid down the door to the floor. My head between my knees, I attempted to get my breathing under control. Please, please let me find Jace. Returning to The Farm was not an option.

I sat still and listened, hoping the house was devoid of soldiers. As soon as I was steady enough to walk, I walked to the kitchen, avoiding the windows to ensure the soldier on the street wouldn't see me. The kitchen hadn't changed since I'd been here last.

And no Jace.

I searched upstairs, standing in reverence in the doorway to the baby's room for a long moment. Still, no Jace.

I needed to think. How did he get in here? I didn't remember hearing a door opening and closing. Last time I was here, he remained in the house after I left. What was it about this house that he kept coming back to? Of course, I kept coming back for sentimental reasons, but was that his reason? He told me not to come back here. If he was just randomly passing through searching for food, why would it matter if I returned to this particular house. Once he'd raided its supplies, it would be of no further use to him.

Unless it served some other purpose.

I found the basement steps. This place had to have a solar flare shelter like my house had. I searched the basement. Inside the furnace room, I found what I was looking for—a heavy door, standard for solar flare shelters. I pressed the button to open the hatch, but it didn't budge. Of course. No electricity.

I opened the panel under the switch to access a hand crank. I expected it to stick after being out of use for so long, but I had no trouble turning it. Cranking the wheel, I watched the door open, darkness beyond it. With it open just enough to squeeze my body through, I stepped inside. Cautiously, I descended the steep stairs into the shelter.

24

More tunnels

BEFORE I CLOSED the hatch to the solar flare shelter and descended into absolute darkness, I searched for a light source. I found a couple of flashlights that still worked, a box of candles, a book of matches, and a few cans of soup. The stockpile wouldn't last more than a couple of days. I'd have to move on after that.

Move on to where?

A burning sensation flooded my chest. I couldn't think about that right now. All that mattered was that I'd escaped The Farm. But what about Dean? What would they do to him? Would they imprison him in the psychiatric ward? No, no they couldn't.

I stared at the still-open hatch door. Should I go back for him?

He could say that I snuck out while he was sleeping. He was genius. I had to believe he'd come up with something.

I lit a candle and set the match, other candles, and flashlights on a tiny metal table beside the cot where I could easily find them if this one went out while I was sleeping. With a deep breath, I cranked the door closed and engaged the lock. A metallic clang echoed around me.

The candle flickered and cast ominous shadows on the concrete walls. My stomach tightened. I'm on my own. Alone. The finality of what I'd done hit me and my heart rate spiked. *No, I'm not going to be afraid.* If I starved out here, it was better than the luxury of the The Farm.

I laid down on the cot. Dust motes clouded my vision and a musty scent irritated my nose. Though beyond exhausted, I couldn't fall asleep. The mattress springs poked me in the back. I rolled over and faced the wall, then rolled back again. I watched the candle burn; the dancing flame mesmerized me and then lulled me to sleep.

Dr. Rail's blood red nails dig into my scaly flesh. Blood pools around them, then drips down my arm.

I gasped and bolted upright on the cot. Thick blackness surrounded me. Images of Dr. Rail formed in the darkness. I scrabbled for the matches and candle. Holding my breath, my hands trembled as I struck the match once, twice, three times. Finally, a spark and a flame caught and illuminated the small room. I held out the tiny light, searching each corner for Dr. Rail, for soldiers.

The room was empty.

I released my breath, lit a candle, and placed it on the bedside table. I rubbed my arm where I could've sworn her claws were really digging into me. But my skin was perfect, though the memory of the pain lingered.

I ran my fingers through my hair. Though still tired, I didn't want to close my eyes again. The nightmare felt only a whisper away.

Footfalls thudded above me. My heart leapt. Could it be Jace? I went to the hatch and pressed my ear to the door. Voices, muffled by the thick metal. Male voices, several of them. They shouted back and forth to each other.

And then I heard a name that sent adrenaline surging through my veins: "Leah Baines."

How did they find me?

I checked the lock to ensure it was engaged. How long would it take them to find the shelter I'd locked myself inside? I couldn't leave. I'd have to pass them to get out of the house. I was trapped down here, sealed in my own tomb.

They called my name over and over.

I blew out the candle, crawled under the cot, and covered my ears. Maybe if they looked inside, they wouldn't see me and think the room is empty. It was my only hope. If they found me, I'd spend the rest of my life drooling in front of that TV in the psych ward.

In the cool, damp darkness, I scooted against the wall and curled myself into a tight ball. Silent, terrifying moments passed.

A breeze of cooler air swept over me. The room lit in dim light. Footsteps. My pulse pounded in my ears. I controlled my breathing, forcing shallow silent breaths. All I could do was stay still and hope they didn't look under the cot.

And then, dusty boots walked to one end of the room and then back. They stopped in front of the cot. The box of matches rattled and then the scraping sound of a match being lit. The room brightened.

"I thought I told you not to come back here." A familiar voice.

The boot wearer dropped to his haunches and peered under the cot.

Jace?

He reached under the cot for me. I stared at his hand. Was it really him? Or was this my imagination again?

"It's okay, Leah."

I opened my mouth to speak, but my voice refused to work.

Jace flashed a gentle smile. "This isn't going to be like the closet, is it?"

"How?" I swallowed to wet my throat. "How'd you get in here?"

"I have my ways. Come on out. Give me your hand."

After a moment's hesitation, I grabbed his hand and he pulled me out from under the cot.

He walked to the hatch and placed his ear against it. Would they still be calling my name?

Seeming satisfied, he turned back to me. "So what did you do to get the lizards so upset?"

"I-I ran away."

He tilted his head and narrowed his eyes. "Why would you do that?"

I glanced down at the floor then back to him. "It's a long story, but I can't go back there."

He sighed and then stared at the wall and then at the shelf on the wall that held the canned goods.

"Jace, was this your house before you went underground?" I asked.

He straightened his back. "No, why do you ask?"

"I'm just wondering why you're always here."

"It's a long story and I'd rather hear yours."

I looked up at the ceiling. "What if they find us?"

"Those guys are strong, but about as smart as their reptilian relatives. It's the silver ones you have to worry about. If they happen to get close, I'll deal with that when it comes. So, tell me this long story and give me a good reason not to send you back to The Farm."

After a silent moment to compose my thoughts, I launched into the story and didn't hold back. I spilled everything—the truth about Dr. Rail, what they expected between Dean and me, the psychiatric ward, and even what Dean was up to with the Zombie Epoch game.

Everything.

By the time I was done, horror twisted Jace's face.

The cot creaked as Jace eased his weight onto it. "It's a breeding facility. They're breeding slaves. Smart slaves, but slaves all the same," he said.

I nodded. I grabbed handfuls of hair and thought back to when this all started—how we had competed with one another for who would get to take the Typhon treatments and live at The Farm. Who would survive as mankind's last remnant.

We competed to be their slaves.

Jace stared ahead, his brow furrowed. He drew choppy breaths as though he was going to say something but then decided against it.

He stood. "Leah, I'm going to take you home with me, but you should know, this may not go well."

"What does that mean?"

"The people I'm with—the other survivors—they don't really like Typhons."

"What will they do?"

"Well, they might be . . ." He rubbed the back of his neck. "They might be upset."

I stepped backward. "Like irritated upset or like kill-me-slowly upset."

"Probably kill-you-quickly upset."

My mouth fell open.

Jace stepped toward me. "But don't worry. I won't let anything happen to you. We'll just have to explain the whole thing."

I sat on the cot and looked up at Jace, weighing my options: get murdered by humans or become another vegetable in the psych ward salad. It was an easy decision. Murder it was.

"So?" he asked.

"I'll follow you."

Jace stepped closer to the shelf that housed the canned foods. He tugged at a can of green beans and something clicked. A slivered opening appeared in the wall. Jace dug his fingers into the crack, pulled, and a door swung open. A cool, musty breeze ruffled my hair. Another dark tunnel stretched beyond the small doorway.

Jace switched on his LED flashlight and illuminated the tunnel. "Let's go."

25

Humans

Aʜᴇᴀᴅ, ᴛʜᴇ ᴛᴜɴɴᴇʟ loomed. Dirt walls, dirt floor and about waist height. The scent of cool, moist earth surrounded me. I glanced backward at the heavy door that led to the house and eventually back to The Farm. What and who were on the other end of this tunnel?

I couldn't go back. My future lay before me—no matter how short that future might be.

Jace blew out my candle and crawled into the tunnel. "You coming or what?"

I nodded and crouched. Jace pressed himself against the dirt wall while I crawled in beside him. He swung the door closed and locked it. Relief washed over me. I breathed in the damp air—it smelled of freedom.

"Let's go," Jace said as he pivoted in the tight space and crawled toward the darkness ahead.

For a few moments, we crept ahead in silence and then Jace stopped. "I'm sorry, Leah."

"Sorry for what? You're helping me."

"I knew what they were and yet I sent you back into the lion's den. I'm sorry."

"You don't have to be sorry. You thought I was one of them." I hung my head and was glad the flashlight lit the tunnel and not me. "I mean, I look like them."

"I see now that you're a victim too. Just like all the rest of us."

147

"Thanks. Thanks for . . ."

"Look, no biggie. Let's get as far as we can from those things."

Jace crawled forward and I followed. I smacked my kneecap on a rock and groaned. "You okay?" Jace asked.

"Yeah, I'm fine."

"Up ahead we're going to go downhill for a little while. When we get to the bottom, we'll be able to walk."

We crawled on. The ground began to slope downward, a gentle descent at first, but then it steepened. I dug my fingernails into the dirt to keep from sliding forward into Jace. We descended deeper into the earth, the air getting colder and the tunnel floor wetter the farther we went.

Jace disappeared through an opening; I crawled after him and came out into a taller tunnel.

I stood up on aching knees and stretched my back. Jace's head was only about a centimetre from the ceiling. He held up the flashlight so I could see my hands. They were blackened from the dirt as were my jeans. Thick, rough-cut wooden beams supported the ceiling in regular intervals.

"Another twenty minutes and we'll be there."

I took in his the creases between his eyebrows. "You look worried."

"I am."

"Should I be worried?"

He sighed. "Probably."

"There are about fifteen others living in the tunnels here besides my dad, my sister and me. My dad is pretty bitter and my sister . . . well," he rubbed the back of his neck. "She's difficult on the best day. I think she could use some sun."

Maybe it should have scared me, but somehow after dealing with Dr. Rail, a bunch of angry humans seemed like a gentle breeze on a warm day.

"Are you okay? Do you still want to come with me?" he asked.

I shrugged. "Bring it, I guess." What did I have to lose? Nothing I'd miss. Couldn't say I wouldn't be relieved to have this life over.

We walked on, Jace taking long strides and me intermittently jogging to keep up. The tunnel floor was more packed here as though well-traveled. Jace slowed and began glancing back at me every few minutes, his brow becoming more and more furrowed. Was he trying to figure out how he would explain my presence, how he would try to convince everyone that he hasn't shown the enemy their secret hideout. If I were him, I'd be super anxious.

I was super anxious and I wasn't him. My bravery was melting away. Murmurs echoed down the tunnel. We both halted. Jace grabbed my hand. "Stay beside me. Let me handle this."

The voices grew louder.

"You don't have to protect me, Jace. I mean, what happens, happens. I'm not afraid."

But my heart thudded in my ears. This could finally be the end.

Jace gripped my hand so tightly my fingers ached. We came to a fork in the tunnel. The voices were clearly coming from the tunnel to the right.

Jace pulled in a deep breath and squared his shoulders. "Let the games begin."

Acid filled my chest. Jace placed himself in front of me. We walked into a large, cave-like room. A group of people sat at a picnic table. None of them seemed to notice us.

A dark-haired girl with colourful wires in her hands glanced up and her gaze locked on Jace and then darted to me. Her mouth fell open and she froze. And then a man noticed her stare and followed her gaze to us. His eyes widened.

Then Jace spoke. "Everyone needs to stay calm."

26

No Calm in this Storm

HOLDING MY BREATH, I inched closer to Jace.

The girl continued to stare and then every other head in the room turned in our direction. Their faces morphed from surprise to red-faced, hard-glaring anger—murderous, seething anger.

"Breathe, Leah. It's going to be okay," he whispered. "And you're cutting off the circulation in my hand."

I loosened my grip, and my fingers ached from squeezing so hard.

One by one, they rose to their feet. The dark-haired girl marched toward us. She glowered at me and then her gaze flashed down to Jace's hand on mine. I shook his hand off. I didn't need to cause any more trouble for him than I already was.

"What in the hell are you doing?" she demanded.

"Leah, this is my sister, Jenna. Jenna, this is Leah."

"I don't want to know its name, Jace. How could you bring it here? You've shown it how to find—"

"Relax, I'm going to explain everything."

Jenna folded her arms. "You've endangered everyone here!"

The others murmured. One boy, maybe twelve or thirteen years old, broke away from the rest and ran down a tunnel at the back. Jenna looked back and then threw

Jace a satisfied smile. Jace squared his shoulders. Moments later, the boy reappeared with an older man beside him. An older Jace.

"Dad is going to kill it. And then you." Jenna shook her head.

Being called "it" made me feel ant sized. But she was right. I was an it—a mutant.

The man I assumed to be Jace's father pushed past the others, his face a glowing molten shade of red. His gaze raked over the little bit of me not hidden behind Jace then the molten red morphed into purple.

Jace stepped back, pushing me back with him. "Uh. Hey, Dad."

The others closed in behind him, fists clenched and jaws tensed.

Long seconds of silence passed punctuated by my heart hammering my ribs passed.

The man lifted his chin. "What in the hell are you thinking bringing that thing in here? It will bring all the lizards down on us! Jenna, go get a rope so we can tie it up. We can't have it getting away."

"No, Dad, she won't tell anyone. She's not one of them," Jace said.

"Well, it sure as hell looks like one!"

Jace straightened his back. "She used to be human."

"Well, it is one of them now."

"Dad, she needs a place to stay. They were going to hurt her. I had to bring her here."

His gaze narrowed. "The silver ones are smart. They know our weaknesses and you, son, played right into its hands."

Jenna returned with some rope. I shouldn't have come here. Of course, they'd never believe I was different from the others. I studied the angry set of Jenna's lips, her soft, pink human lips. A heavy weight fell into my stomach. What I wouldn't give to be human like her. Instead, I was this . . . this thing.

Jace's father turned to her. "Go pat it down. Make sure it doesn't have any weapons or tracking devices."

Jace blocked her. "You don't need to do that, Jenna."

She side-stepped him. She ran her hand up and down either side of me and then she grabbed my wrist and examined my watch. "All she's got is a watch."

"Smash it," his dad barked. "It's probably got a tracking device in it."

She tugged at the band. I tore my arm away. Not Dad's watch. It was all I had left of him. "Don't touch me!"

"Cooperate lizard," Jenna said.

I stared into her eyes. "You can do what you want to me, but you can't take my watch."

"Jace make it give me the watch," Jenna said. "It doesn't want us to have it for a reason."

"Leah, maybe just let her look at the watch, so she can see you're not hiding anything," Jace said.

"Yeah, so I can smash it." Jenna held out her hand. "Give it to me. Now!"

"No!" I shouted. "The only way you're getting it is to cut it off my dead body."

"It would be my pleasure, lizard." Jenna grabbed my arm.

Jace pushed his sister back. "Just let me explain this before anyone kills anyone."

His dad reached around his back and brought out a handgun. "Sure. Okay. Jace, you tell us its sob story and then we'll kill it."

"You're not going to kill her," Jace said.

"If it puts us in danger, I will kill it." He waved his hand. "Well, let's hear the lies it told you."

Jace relayed the story I'd told him and the reasons I couldn't go back to the project. Jenna stood with her arms folded and rolled her eyes a few times.

His dad scratched the back of his head. "That's quite the story. How do I know any of it is true?"

"I trust her." Jace sighed. "She's not lying." Jace's reasoning was flimsy at best. If I was in their shoes, I probably wouldn't buy it either. But why did he believe me? It wasn't as though he knew me that well. So we'd met a couple of times. It wasn't enough to know if we could trust one another or not.

Though, here I was trusting him with no good reason why either.

His dad looked at me. "You've been awfully quiet, letting my son speak for you. Your kind stole everything from us, and you want me to feed you and put a roof over your head."

His accusations stung, but the part about me stealing everything unleashed a bomb of hot anger in my chest. "I didn't steal anything from you. They stole everything from us."

His dad's brow drew together. "Don't lump me in with you and your kind."

"My kind? I was like you. And don't tell me what you lost! You still have your son and your daughter, your friends—you're still human. I lost everything. Everything! Both parents, my sister, my friends. And look at me." I waved my hand over my body. "They made me into a monster!"

He leaned back against the dirt wall. "Prove it. If you're one of us, then prove it."

I bristled. "How am I supposed to do that?"

He smirked. "I don't know. You're the smart one. Figure it out."

Jace shifted his weight. "Dad—"

"Son, it wants to stay. I need a little proof."

I wracked my brain. The only thing I had left of my human life was the watch Dad gave me—the one they wanted to smash. It wasn't definitive, but it was my only hope.

"My dad was a navy pilot. His plane went down over the Persian Gulf five years ago." I held up the watch for him to see. "He left me his watch. If you look up his obituary it will have me listed as his daughter. He's wearing this watch in the picture. His name was Jordan Baines."

Jace's dad's eyes widened and he blinked a couple of times. Then his smug façade crumbled. Did I convince him? Hope inflated inside me, but his gaze turned hard again.

"Of course you know that name. You'd have me believe you are Jordan Baines's daughter?" He spoke of him as though he knew him.

"He was your dad?" Jace asked, awe saturating his voice.

His dad glared at me. "It's making up stories, Jace."

Jace threw up his hand to stop him from speaking and turned to me.

"Do you know him?" I asked Jace, ignoring the purple-faced man that looked like he was about to explode.

"I know of him. We all do. He was a whistleblower. He was able to tell a few people about the aliens before they killed him. Of course, most people didn't believe him. They thought it was some crazy conspiracy theory. But we went underground. If it weren't for him, it would have been too late by the time we realized what was going on."

Jace turned to his dad. "If you don't let her stay, I'm leaving with her."

"You wouldn't last a week out there on your own, son."

"It's both of us or neither of us," Jace said.

His dad huffed out a heavy breath. "You can move through their tunnels, can't you?"

I nodded.

"You want me to believe that you're not a threat and that you're on our side?"

I nodded again, but a sick feeling settled into the pit of my stomach.

His dad rubbed his chin. "How about a little test of your loyalty? To see whose side you're really on?"

27

The Test

"**T**HERE ARE HEAT sensors in the tunnel. A human goes in there, alarms go off. You run about five degrees cooler. If you go in, no alarms," Jace's dad said.

"Dad, no." Jace shook his head.

"Jace, we've been trying to figure out a way to get in there. Now we've got one." Then he turned to me. "I want you to destroy the coil. With the coil gone, humans have a fighting chance."

My mouth dropped open. He may as well have asked me to fly. "How am I supposed to do that?"

"With a bomb."

Jace stepped between me and his dad. "No. No! You can't send her back there."

"She'll take the service tunnel directly under the coil. She'll secure and activate the bomb. Then she'll have five minutes to get out. When the coil goes up in flames, she'll be one of us and she can live here."

Now that he had a use for me he called me "she."

"No, it's too dangerous. I guess we're leaving then," Jace said.

His dad was right. I knew my way around the tunnels. I even knew my way around the coil building. If the coil was destroyed it would set everything right. I remembered my mom's words: "Be a good girl and save the world." Maybe this is why I was saved.

"I'll do it," I said.

Jace squeezed my hand. "No, you won't."

"Tell me what I need to do."

28

Neither Human nor Typhon

I FOLLOWED JACE'S dad down another corridor and Jace followed me. He led me into a room full of electronics: most of it was older than me, but there were a few modern pieces. A table sat at the center of the room, strewn with wires and disembodied mother boards. His dad went to a metal cabinet that stood against a wall. He dug a key out of his pocket and wriggled it into the pad lock. The doors clambered as he threw them open.

He pulled a football-sized contraption off a high shelf and brought it to the table, cradling it in his arms. With both hands he eased it down onto the table.

"Dad, I'll do this. I'll go," Jace said.

"You know you can't get through those tunnels. So you either shut up or you leave."

I reached out for Jace's hand. I didn't want him to go. He threaded his fingers through mine and stayed at my side.

"You'll need to secure this to the base of the coil," his dad began. "It's pretty simple. It has magnets on the back to hold it in place." He pointed to two long black strips that ran down one side of the device. "Flipping this switch activates it. Once it's activated you won't be able to turn it off. The ignition is wired into the magnets so if they try to remove it, it'll blow. Once it's live, you'll have five minutes to get out of there before it goes off."

"Can't you give her more time?" Jace asked.

His dad glared at him. "We can't risk the lizards disabling it or moving it. Five minutes is already too much time."

I could see he would prefer a kamikaze bomber.

He went back to the cabinet and retrieved a bag. He carefully stowed the bomb in the green canvas backpack, threw in a roll of duct tape, and handed the bag to me. "Don't blow yourself up." Then he walked out of the room. The last glimpse I caught of him told me he didn't expect to see me again.

Jace took the pack out my hands and set it on the table. "Let's leave. Let's get out of here. I shouldn't have brought you here. I should have known . . ."

"I have to do this. I'm meant to do this," I said. "If I die. I die." I thought of my mom's words again—save the world—and the memory brought tears to my eyes. I sucked in a ragged breath. "My dad's asleep. My mom's asleep. Lindsay is asleep. And I'm so tired, Jace."

I pushed away my tears. Jace wrapped his arms around me. I tensed. How could someone like him stand to touch someone like me? But as his warmth cocooned around me, I melted into him. I rested my head on his shoulder and tried to make it another one of those memories that's etched permanently in my brain. I breathed him in, his wonderful human scent. I relished the warmth rolling off him and promised myself I would always remember.

"Will you help me find my way back to the tunnel?" I asked, tearing up again.

"Of course," Jace said. "I will try to talk you out of it on the way."

"Please don't."

Jace stroked away another one of my tears.

The Typhon Project

"Let's go," I said.

Jace led me back down the tunnel we'd not long ago come down to get to the survivors' hideout. Not long ago, though somehow it seemed like weeks ago. The pack hung heavy on my shoulder. The bomb. I carried a bomb that could wipe out Jace and me in an instant.

Jace walked ahead. Periodically, he glanced back at me, eyes wide and brow furrowed by the light of his flashlight. Was he sad or angry? I didn't know. Why would he be sad or angry? If I die, I'll just be one less Typhon to threaten his world.

I wished I could be something else. One or the other. Instead, I was both. Inside, human. Outside, Typhon. But no one cared about the inside. They only cared about what they saw—reptilian pupils, scaly skin.

Maybe the human me and the Typhon me would both die today.

When we made it to the door into the house, Jace pressed his finger to his lips. Not that I'd made any noise up to that point. "You wait here," he whispered. "I'm going to make sure it's empty."

Why should he risk himself for me? I shook my head. "I'll do it," I whispered back. I stepped forward, and he grasped my shoulder.

His nostrils flared. "I said, I'll do it."

I lifted my chin. He pointed at me; his gaze bore into mine.

Fine. I'd let him do it.

He slipped through the door and closed it behind him. With the flashlight gone, I was plunged into total darkness. I strained my ears to hear what was happening on the other side of the metal door, but the silence was as impenetrable as the darkness.

Please let him be okay. Please let him be okay. Please.

I couldn't take knowing one of the last humans died to save me.

The door squeaked open and Jace and his flashlight reappeared. "All clear."

I put up my hand and squinted against the flashlight.

He lowered it and said, "Come on."

I stepped inside the solar flare shelter and then Jace closed the door. I turned around to face him. "Thanks, for helping me get back. I can take it from here."

"No, it's okay." He shrugged. "I'll make sure you make it back to the tunnel okay."

I hoisted the pack higher on my shoulder. "You don't need to risk yourself for me. Just . . . leave."

"This is my fault. I shouldn't have taken you there."

"Don't worry about it. Have a good life." I spun around and headed farther into the house. Jace's footsteps thumped behind me. Tears stung my eyes. Why couldn't he just go? Why did he have to act like he cared? It made me feel worse—all pink and soft and vulnerable. Every human part of me raged. Hot blooded and afraid.

I climbed the stairs out of the basement and was back on the main floor of the house that could've been mine. It was still dark, but sunrise would come soon. I walked into the living room to scan the area once more before venturing outside. I peered out of the large picture window. I could see the manhole from here, a blemish in the asphalt.

"Why did you come to *this* house the first time?" Jace's voice startled me.

I glanced back at him, standing in the doorway to the basement stairs.

I stared at him for a moment. The reason was so personal, embarrassing even. But, likely, I was about to die. What did I have to lose? I sighed. "I just wanted to get away from the Farm. And this place looks like my house, the one I grew up in." I swallowed hard. "I was pretending I was home, talking to my family. Lindsay and I always used fight over the pop tarts. It seems like a stupid thing to fight over now."

Jace stepped closer. "That's what siblings do, isn't it? Fight over stupid things? My brother and I . . . we used to. . ." He looked down. "Never mind."

He shuffled to my side and pinned his stare on the street. "You don't have to do this. You could just go back and resume your life there. What's my dad going to do about it?"

"I gave my word."

"Under duress."

"I promised my mom that I'd save the world."

"It might not work," he said.

I squared my shoulders; I wanted to be strong. "No one will know until I try. Maybe it will work and you guys would have a fighting chance."

Memories of Dean helping me leave the project flooded back. Had they already figured out I was gone? Would he be punished? Especially after I set a bomb.

"Jace, I need you to listen carefully. There's a boy at The Farm named Dean Green. He knows everything about the coil, and he's on your side. You can trust him." I blew out a trembling breath. "If I fail and they haven't discovered he helped me escape, he might be able to help. There's this game they play called Zombie Epoch on Tynet. If you can hack in, you can communicate with him."

Jace nodded in tight movements.

What else did I need to tell him? A feeling in the pit of my stomach told me these were my final words. My throat tightened. I lifted my wrist and stared at my watch—Dad's watch. The compass needle meandered. I loosened it from my wrist. "Can you look after this for me?" I held the watch out to him.

He took a step back. "You might need that."

"I don't want it to get damaged. It's important to me."

He reached out and took it from me. "You're coming back, you know. I'll be waiting for you here."

I licked my lips. "You should go home in case the soldiers come back."

He squeezed the watch in his fist. "No, I'll see you back here in a couple hours."

I picked up his wrist. I watched for a shudder at my cool, scaly touch, but it didn't come. I took the watch out of his hand and buckled it onto his wrist. "Take care, Jace."

I walked to the front door and grabbed the knob.

"I'll see you later," he called after me.

"Goodbye, Jace." I opened the door and stepped out into the frigid night air. I looked up and down the street for good measure and then darted to the manhole cover, pulled it off, and climbed inside. I fixed the cover in place then descended the ladder.

The tunnel stretched in front of me. At the other end was the Tesla coil. I pulled the pack straps over both shoulders, tightened them, and broke into a run.

The bomb pressed into my back. This was why I was saved. I was sure of it.

29

Panic and Courage

AT FIRST, I was worried the backpack bouncing as I ran would detonate the bomb, but after a couple minutes, I relaxed. My feet slapped the cement as my long strides carried me closer to The Farm. I no longer wanted to slow this down. I wanted it to be over.

When I reached the usual shaft inside The Farm's boundaries, I passed it by. I followed the tunnel in a direction I'd never gone before. I'd only tried to escape The Farm; never tried to go deeper into it. The tunnel ran beneath the coil. I had a strong suspicion there would be another shaft that led up and into the Tesla Coil building. If there was, I wouldn't have to risk being seen by a surveillance camera.

Dean flashed in my thoughts. Would they have discovered me gone? I swallowed hard. What would they do to him if they found out he was involved? I slowed my pace as my thoughts spiralled. If they hurt him because of me . . .

I couldn't live with myself.

I wouldn't be alive much longer anyway.

"I'm sorry, Dean," I breathed.

Ahead, another shaft came into view. I stopped at the ladder and peered up at the hatch above.

You can do this.

I had to. If this worked, Jace and the other survivors might have a fighting chance. If it didn't work, I'd have died for nothing. My life didn't mean much to me with my family and the body I used to know gone, but I still wanted my life to matter. I promised Mom.

Please let this work.

I climbed the ladder up to the hatch, put my shoulder into it, and shoved. But it didn't open. I climbed one rung higher and pushed with my legs. The thing didn't budge as if it was welded shut. I tried again, straining until my muscles burned, but I couldn't get it to move.

I climbed back down the ladder and stared up at the hatch. I grabbed handfuls of my hair and pulled, nearly dislodging my wig. My breathing came in shallow gasps. I was counting on that entry point. Now, my only option was to use the hatch in the lawn and go in through the main doors.

My chances were grim before, but I'd held onto a glimmer of hope that I could get in without getting caught. That option was dead. In going through the front doors, I had to pass cameras. They would know I was there, and they would come after me. Using those doors assured me of either capture or death. Or both.

I climbed back up the ladder to the coil building hatch and reefed on it a couple more times. Please open. My shoulder throbbed by the time I gave up.

It wasn't going to open.

My heart sank. I collapsed to the floor of the tunnel and buried my head in my hands. Getting captured was not an option. If I continued on my mission, there was only one option left for me: I go down with the coil. I'd walk inside and detonate the thing before they could get to me and stop me.

I forced myself to my feet. I hurried to the other shaft. I had to do this before I lost my nerve. I climbed the ladder and flipped open the hatch. After checking for witnesses, I scurried onto the perfectly-manicured grass and closed the hatch. A sliver of sun peeked over the horizon. So beautiful but so deadly. This was the last time I would see it.

Goodbye.

I ran to the coil building and, keeping to the shadows, skulked toward the front of the building.

My next step would take me within range of the cameras. I had to move fast. Once they caught sight of me, I'd only have minutes. I put my head down and sprinted around the front of the building. I slid to a stop in front of the glass doors and pressed my thumb to the black box. The door buzzed and clicked. I paused, looked up at the camera, and smiled.

I threw the door open and bolted for the second access point. I pressed my thumb to another box and shoved the steel door open. I darted for the coil while the steel door crashed closed behind me. The coil lay in front of me. I slid my backpack off as I ran and ripped open the zipper. Stopping at the steel undergirding that held up the immense coil, I yanked the duct tape out of the bag as the coil thrummed with energy. I glanced around. So far no one had found me.

I peeled a length of tape off the roll and tore it off with my teeth. I dug the bomb out of the bag and pressed it against the steel supports. Holding it in place with my leg, I fixed it to the girder.

A metal-grating screech echoed around me. The door! Someone was here. Then heavy footfalls—boots on cement.

Typhon soldiers spilled through the door. I reached for the detonator switch and five lasers converged on my chest.

"Don't move. Put your hands up!" A voice boomed.

I froze with my finger on the switch. "Put your guns down or else I'll arm it!"

The lasers centered over my heart, but my finger remained on the switch. I eyed the crocodilian faces of the soldiers, their yellow eyes squinting into the sights of their guns.

"If you lower your guns I'll come with you quietly," I shouted.

No one moved. My pulse rushed in my ears and my legs went numb.

A clicking sound broke the silence. Click, clack. Click, clack. Growing closer every moment.

And then Dr. Rail stepped in front of the soldiers. "You don't want to do that, Leah. In fact, if you tell us where you got it we might be able to overlook all of this."

I glared at her and kept my finger on the switch.

She smiled. "You don't want to die, Leah. Just step away from it. This is all a big mistake."

I ground my teeth together.

Dr. Rail took a step forward.

"Don't come any closer!" I shouted.

"I'm glad you came back, Leah. This is where you belong. That looks like a human contraption. Did they put you up to this?"

She took another step toward me. "You see how they are? You used to be one of them and they treat you like this? Sending you to die for their cause. Leah, just put the device down."

I peered into her eyes. "No."

She smirked. "Bring him in," she called over her shoulder.

A soldier shoved a boy through the door. A bloody and swollen face, unrecognizable. Then his gaze met mine with the one eye that wasn't swollen shut. Dean! "What did you do to him?" I said.

Dr. Rail sighed. "He refused to tell us where you disappeared to. This all works out well though. See, he still has a use."

The soldier nudged Dean forward with the barrel of his gun. Dean stumbled.

She walked over to Dean, dug her fingernails into his scalp, and yanked his head back. "You step away from that or Dean dies."

Tears blurred my eyes. I glanced between my friend and the bomb. Would they let him live if I gave up?

Could I trust anything Dr. Rail said? The defunct magnetic field, them changing us into Typhons, the purpose of The Farm—all lies. They'd kill Dean. If they didn't kill me, they'd turn me into a vegetable and lock me in the psych ward.

"Dean—I'm so sorry," I said.

"It's okay," he said. I noticed him square his shoulders. "Leah?"

He locked his gaze on me and nodded.

"Flip the switch," Dean said.

A chest pounding boom split the air. Dean lurched forward and fell to his knees. Blood spread across the chest of his shirt and he fell face down to the floor.

"No!" I shouted. Dr. Rail smirked.

I flipped the switch. Another shot rang out. Something threw me backward, like I'd been smacked in the shoulder with a baseball bat. I threw my hand over my shoulder. A warm fluid oozed between my fingers. I stumbled sideways and fell to the floor. I looked up at the bomb. Red digital numbers counted down.

30

Alien Liar

DR. RAIL HOVERED over me, staring wide-eyed at the bomb strapped to one of the Tesla Coil's support beams.

"Get someone in here to disable this!" Dr. Rail shouted.

Stars scattered across my vision. I held up my hand. Blood. Blackness began closing in. I pulled in a breath. My shoulder burned. The rest of me was numb. Voices shouted but grew more and more distant. No. No! I pushed at the darkness. I hung on to consciousness by a thread. A Typhon ran in. I lay between him and Dr. Rail, staring up at them. I recognized him. One of the scientists who worked on the coil. He started fidgeting with the bomb. The time read four minutes.

"I think it's this one," he said.

"Do it," she said.

"I can't be sure, though. I—"

Dr. Rail glowered at him. "I said do it!"

I wanted to stop him. I opened my mouth but couldn't find my voice. I felt like I was being pulled under water and it would just be easier to sink.

But I held on.

The scientist yanked a wire. The clock flashed and stopped. Dr. Rail's lips curled into a cruel grin.

But the countdown started again.

Two minutes.

"Get everyone out of here," the scientist said as he backed away from the explosive.

"Everyone out!" Dr. Rail screeched.

A soldier took a step toward me. Dr. Rail grabbed the soldier's sleeve. "Leave those two here."

Boots stomped on the floor. The heavy door opened. The footfalls ebbed away. The door slammed.

Silence.

I cranked my neck so I could see Dean. Pain shot out of my shoulder and exploded in my head. I pulled in a ragged breath. Dean lay perfectly still in a pool of blood.

Tears swelled in the corners of my eyes. They dribbled down my temple and mixed with the pool of blood that was forming under me. It's my fault he's dead.

A bang rang out, muffled and distant. It didn't matter. Nothing mattered except that I got Dean killed.

The illuminated numbers ticked downward. One minute left. "I'm sorry, Dean." I tried to say it loud enough for him to hear if he was still alive, but it was nothing more than a whisper. Just a little longer and it would all be over.

At least, maybe Dean died for something—I'd die for something. I succeeded. I honoured my mother's last request. Peace settled over me like a warm blanket.

My vision narrowed and darkened until the glow of numbers were at the end of a gray tunnel. Would it hurt to die?

A voice calling my name. But it was far away. "Leah, Leah," it said as though it was calling me home. Was it Dad? I was tired. So tired and so cold. I'm coming, Dad. I stopped trying to hang on. I let go. I plummeted into darkness.

Pain. So much pain!

The Typhon Project

I cried out and opened my eyes. My head throbbed. My shoulder burned. Everything's wrong. I saw plaid. And walls. I couldn't make sense of it. I was going down, down, down.

"Run!" The voice yelled.

A jolt and bouncing, my stomach took the brunt. I cried out again. What was happening?

Lifting my head required all my strength. Cement walls. Lights. The tunnel?

A boom tore through the tunnel.

"Faster!" the voice shouted.

It felts like the air has been sucked out of the chamber. A high-pitched keening.

Light flashed behind us as we barrelled through the tunnel. Heat blasted against me. I lifted my head enough to see a fireball chasing us.

31

Dean's Fate

SOMEONE CARRIED ME over their shoulder. I bounced as they sprinted away from the inferno travelling toward us like a freight train. Thuds and cracks rang out amidst a thunderous roar. The fire, like a predator, pursued us to devour us. Pain wrapped my body with every bounce. I held my breath. I survived the initial blast—somehow. Now I would die in the tunnel.

"Up here!" a voice I'd never heard said, barely audible above the roar of the blaze.

Another thud. This one in front of us. Another.

"Hurry!" shouted the one who carried me. As fear cleared my head, the voice became familiar. Jace. Jace?

Another boom. The fire reached out its scorching tentacles. The heat burned my lungs.

Jace bolted sideways and then we were falling and sliding into darkness. Orange light followed us then a thud and the light disappeared. My head smacked something solid. A moment of pain. My head swam and then—

It hurt. I was breathing. Breathing hurt. I tried to make sense of it. My head throbbed. Every beat of my heart was echoed in my shoulder. I was just a head and a shoulder. Nothing else.

Then there were voices. Far away voices. Yelling, but they sounded . . . happy.

Happy?

It was dark, no, not dark. Red. Something blocked the red and then it was black. Then it went red again. I tried opening my eyes. My eyelids were heavy. Heavy as manhole covers. I heaved them open, but the effort exhausted me, and they closed before I could make sense of anything. I drifted into sleep and then out of sleep and then back into it again.

A warm hand and a voice. "Leah?" the voice that was calling me home. Fingers on the back of my hand. I wiggled the fingers on that hand. A lightning bolt of pain. I gasped.

"Leah, wake up."

I forced my eyelids open, but everything was blurry. I blinked hard and then squinted, trying to focus them.

"Leah."

I looked toward the voice. A face came into focus. A smile. A bandage wrapped around his forehead.

"Jace," I whispered, my voice as reluctant as my eyes.

He lifted my hand and held it between his warm palms.

"Where?" I couldn't complete the question.

"You're with us."

"Humans?"

"Yeah."

A relieved sigh and then I slowly turned my head and glanced around the room. Dirt walls. Rough beams overhead. The tunnels.

I turned back to Jace. A crease cut deep between his brows. "What's wrong?"

"I was worried about you," he said.

"I thought I was going to die in the coil."

He squeezed my hand. "I couldn't let that happen." One side of his mouth lifted in a crooked smile.

"You came and got me?"

"Yeah, I barely got us out of the blast zone before the thing went off. I've never run so fast in my life."

"What happened to your head?" I tried raising my arm to point, but a stab of pain shot through me, and I let it drop.

"Just some flying debris, nothing serious."

Memories started to return to me, vivid snapshots.

"The bomb. What happened to the coil?" I asked.

"Nothing but a crater now."

"They shot me."

"You're going to be okay. It went straight through. Didn't hit any major arteries."

I gasped and my throat tightened as another memory flashed. "They shot Dean."

Jace's eyes narrowed. "Dean?"

"Yeah, he was lying on the floor a couple of meters away from me."

Jace shook his head. "No, you were the only one there. Everyone else had cleared the building."

"They shot him in the chest. They left him there to die."

"Leah, I would have seen him if he had been that close to you. Maybe he wasn't hurt as bad as you thought. Maybe he was able to get himself out."

I tensed. How could he not have seen Dean? "I know he was there." I lifted my head off the pillow but winced as stars shot across my vision.

Jace placed his hand on my good shoulder. "You need to relax."

"Is she awake?" A woman's voice called from the door.

Jenna stood in the doorway. I couldn't say I was happy to see her.

"Yeah, she just woke up," Jace said.

She smiled at me. A smile? And it looked genuine. What was wrong with her?

"You'll never guess where I was." She glanced from me to Jace. "I was outside. During. The. Day. First time in five years and let me tell you it was wicked awesome."

I gasped. "It worked?"

Jace dug into his pocket and pulled out Dad's watch. He held it up in front of me. "Your compass points south now. See."

The needle no longer meandered like a lost puppy. It locked on one direction. Tears flooded my eyes. I don't think I'd ever seen such a beautiful sight.

"I'm going back outside," Jenna said as she spun around.

"Hey, be careful. The Typhons are still out there," Jace called.

"Always." She took a step forward then stopped and turned back. "Oh, yeah, and Leah, sorry for the whole 'it' thing."

"That's okay," I said before she disappeared around the corner.

Jace pressed the watch into my palm. "You need to get some sleep, okay?"

I didn't want to sleep anymore, but I was exhausted. "We won."

"Kinda," he said.

"Kinda?"

"The battle has only begun. Typhons won't give up that easy. But what you did gives us a fighting chance." He touched my cheek. "By the way . . . welcome home." He walked out of the room.

I listened as his footsteps grew more and more distant. Maybe the Typhon invasion wasn't the end of the world. If there were survivors here, there might be survivors elsewhere. Maybe I hadn't survived the end of the world.

Maybe this was only the beginning.

About the Author

Melinda Marshall was born in Portland, Oregon, but has spent the past 30 years in Manitoba, Canada.

She has four adult children, two dogs, and enjoys a peaceful life with her partner, a fellow author. In her spare time, she ruminates on all the ways the future could go wrong.

Melinda writes dystopian and science fiction stories, lightly peppered with romance for young people and the young at heart. She authored the *One Bright Future* series.

Also by Melinda Marshall

The One Bright Future series

Enslavement
Subversion
Strategem

The Solar Saga

Solar

Other Fiction

The High-maintenance Ladies of the
Zombie Apocalypse (with Christine Steendam)

Solar

A new story by **Melinda Marshall** coming soon

Chapter One—Beware of Sharks

I'd been waiting a week for the package to arrive.

On my way home from school, I stopped at the cluster of mailboxes, unlocked our box, and peeked inside the dark hole. Just bills and ads. A disappointed sigh, and I pulled out the mail. A key dropped from the bundle and fell to my feet. My enthusiasm rallied. I picked it up. Dry leaves, carried on the breeze, skittered past my black ballet flats as I wriggled the key into the slot on one of the oversized parcel compartments. A textbook shaped package addressed to Haley Klein. It's here!

I added it to the mail pile and glanced toward home a block away. Too excited to wait, I ripped open the cardboard packaging. The title gleamed in burgundy lettering—*Human Genetic Mutation and Variation*. Maybe this one finally held the answers I'd spent the past four years looking for. I wanted to drop onto the sidewalk and start reading, but I strode home, eager for the privacy of my bedroom where I could pour over its pages.

I lugged the mail and my overloaded backpack up my front walk. A moving truck sat on the house next door's driveway and men in navy blue coveralls hauled boxes into the garage. The glossy *SOLD* sticker had appeared on the realty sign a couple of days ago.

I shuffled into the house to find Mom perched in the front window wearing a pair of vacuum-sealed-on jeans and a T-shirt just big enough for a five-year-old. Her smartphone vibrated in circles on the coffee table.

She took a sip from the silver can of diet soda clutched between her electric blue nails. "Did you see the new neighbours are moving in?" she asked without peeling her stare from the window.

"Yep. Hard to miss." The phone stopped dancing for a moment, then started again. "Are you going to answer that?"

She waved her hand. "Nah, it's Roger. I told him it's over, and he seems to think I was kidding."

Roger, the tax attorney. Couldn't say I was sad to be rid of him. "He smelled like sausage."

She glanced back at me and wrinkled her nose. "I know."

Like flashing something shiny in front of a baby, her attention returned to the movers next door.

"Mail," I said, dropping the bundle on the coffee table beside her phone.

"Anything good?"

"Bills, ads. Nothing from Dad."

She looked over her shoulder at the mail pile and frowned. I hurried for the stairs, the new book tucked under my arm.

"They really like grey, and you should've seen the weird painting they carried in." She lifted the can to her lips, slurped. "How much do you think they paid for that place?"

I stopped, my foot on the first step. "I don't know." And I didn't care. All I cared about was getting upstairs and cracking open my new book.

Mom grabbed her phone, tapped the screen, and held it to her ear. Probably calling her realtor friend. I bounded up the stairs two at a time, her intrusive questions following me to the second floor. "That much!"

I swung my bedroom door closed, tethered my phone to a tiny black speaker, and settled onto my bed with my new read. I had physics homework, but that would have to wait. I scoured the book for the next couple of hours, every chapter heading, subtitle, and article that seemed even remotely related to my problems.

Each genetic mutation I read about caused some sort of disability—not enhanced abilities. The farther I moved through the book, the more my heart plummeted.

When I came to the end, I slammed it shut. Another dead end. No closer to finding out what's wrong with me. I was starting to think the only way I'd see headlines about ultra-fast runners or instant healers or fire starters was if I bought a comic book. I groaned. Maybe Mom stood too close to the microwave when she was pregnant with me.

I slid the bulky text onto my bookshelf with the rest of my collection of genetics books and journals, all equally as useless as this new one.

I lay back on my bed and combed my fingers through my hair. Angry tears licked the corners of my eyes.

The smell of frying onions drifted into the room and turned my stomach. I stripped off my school clothes and slipped into a pair of black running shorts and a plain grey Tee, then tiptoed down the stairs amidst the sizzle of the frying pan. If I could just get out before Mom noticed . . .

In the entryway, I shoved my feet into my running shoes and opened the door.

"Haley!"

I ground my teeth.

"Where are you going? It's almost dinner time." Mom's voice carried from the kitchen.

I gripped the doorknob. "For a run!"

"After dinner."

"Just a short one."

"You're eating when you get back, then."

I shook my head. "Fine."

I hurried outside, slamming the door behind me, then jogged down the street.

I made the turn into the park. Though I ached to run, I made one painfully slow lap around the mulched pathway to ensure the park was empty of witnesses. I stopped, activated the stopwatch on my phone, hit the start button, and took off. I sped over the path, the trees blurring to smudges of green and brown. The cooling afternoon air, saturated with the scent of earth and pine, whipped stray strands of my hair back. My breathing grew measured and even, meditative. Worries fell away. The past disappeared. No pressure. No rules. No secrets.

I lengthened my stride and pushed myself harder, intent on breaking my old record. The path looped around and brought me back to the trail head. I slowed to a stop and checked my time. A smile broke loose. Yes! I ran the five-kilometer trail in four minutes and thirty-two seconds—that's a three second improvement. I did a quick mental calculation—66 km/hr. I was getting faster. Was that a good thing or not? Did I want to be any faster than I already was?

I jogged out of the park at normal-person speed, which felt like a crawl, and too soon jogged onto my driveway and back into the house.

I kicked off my running shoes, then bounded into the kitchen for a drink of water. Mom sat at the table before an empty but dirty plate, flipping through one of her magazines. A collage exposed pictures of movie stars with cottage-cheese cellulite popping out of their thighs.

I filled a glass with water from the tap in the fridge door.

She looked up at me and lifted her eyebrows, so I collected a plate, ambled to the counter, and slopped a spoonful of some sort of casserole onto my plate.

After I muscled down the casserole, I returned to my room and cranked my music. I worked on my physics homework and periodically scowled at the new but useless book.

The doorbell rang. Mom's feet thumped toward the door. I turned down the volume down and listened. Vague murmurs followed by Mom's high-pitched cackle echoed up the stairs.

"Haley, could you come down here?" Mom's voice dripped honey.

I slid off my bed and shuffled down the stairs. Our visitor had Mom excited. Never a good sign. There'd probably be a "Well, aren't you grown up" or cheek pinching or worse—an unsolicited hug.

"Haley!" Irritation replaced the sweetness in her voice.

I rounded the corner into the entryway. "I'm right here."

Three strange men stood in the entryway. My breath caught and a cold chill rippled through me, raising every hair on my body. I froze, eyes wide and muscles tensed. It was like I was in the water, cut and bleeding with three sharks circling me. Any moment they might taste blood and devour me. One instinct drowned all others—

Run.

Put as much distance between me and them as possible.

www.ingramcontent.com/pod-product-compliance
Lightning Source LLC
Chambersburg PA
CBHW061444210726

48287CB00007B/2344